Devil's Food Cake and Death

A BEE'S BAKERY COZY MYSTERY BOOK 3

ROSIE A. POINT

You're invited!

Hi there, reader!

I'd like to formally invite you to join my awesome community of readers. We love to chat about cozy mysteries, cooking, and pets.

It's super fun because I get to share chapters from yet-to-be-released books, fun recipes, pictures, and do giveaways with the people who enjoy my stories the most.

So whether you're a new reader or you've been enjoying my stories for a while, you can catch up with other like-minded readers, and get lots of cool content by visiting my website at *www.rosiepointbooks.com* and signing up for my mailing list.

Or simply search for me on *www.bookbub.com* and follow me there.

I look forward to getting to know you better.

Let's get into the story!

Yours,
Rosie

One

"IT'S QUIET. TOO QUIET." THE VOICE RASPED through the door to the bakery kitchen, so sudden and unexpected, that I dropped the wooden spoon I'd been using to mix the cupcake batter.

I was certain, for the briefest moment, that I had imagined it. But of course, I hadn't—the only time I was tired enough to imagine anything was when Ruby woke me up at the crack of dawn to bake. Or when I deigned to drink coffee.

Neither of those events had come to pass today.

Besides, the decorative—and rather annoying—clock on the kitchen wall told me it was just past 06:00 p.m.. Too early to be having fits of tired auditory hallucinations.

I wiped my hands off on my apron, narrowing my eyes at the kitchen door. "Who's out there?" I called sharply.

"Hello? There's someone in here?" The rasp came again.

I marched out of the kitchen and into the bakery, irritation bubbling in my gut. This was meant to be my "alone" time before the end of the day. Ruby had gone home to spend time with Jamie, and I had seen Leslie to the door with a promise that I didn't need any help.

These days, I didn't get a lot of time to bake for pleasure because of how busy the bakery got during the day. And baking was usually when I came up with my best ideas and creative solutions to problems.

I had a big one to solve. One that had developed over the past six months—since before Christmas and Ruby and Jamie's wedding last year.

"Where did you come from?" the voice asked.

A woman who reminded me of a Pineapple Upside-down Cake—ostentatiously dressed and wearing an expression sickly sweet—hovered between the tables in our bakery.

"I'll ask you the same question," I said, walking to the doors of the bakery and brushing past her. She wasn't a customer when we were already closed. She was an intruder, and I didn't recognize her from around Mystery.

"I came for cake," she said. "I heard there's a special on Devil's Food Cake to celebrate the start of summer."

I theorized that summer was the time for Devil's Food

Cake because it was the time when people got up to the most mischief. Myself included.

"Just because you want cake doesn't mean you're going to get it," I said, marveling at my own wisdom. The truth was, I wasn't going to have the cake I wanted either, not in the metaphorical or literal sense.

That was the problem. The root cause stemming from none other than—

"Look, I'm a hungry customer, and I'm new around here so why don't you—?"

"Where are you from?" I found myself unduly curious about her—strange since she had broken the rules. Then again, it had been months since Ruby and I had encountered a good mystery to sink our teeth into.

"New York," she said.

A sharp edge of pain stroked across my heart. Any mention of the city or state brought back memories I'd have preferred to keep locked away.

"And what's your name?"

"Susan Clark," said the Pineapple Upside-down Cake woman.

"Well, Susan Clark from New York," I said, "I'm one hundred percent certain that breaking and entering is a crime where you're from, as it is here. We're closed, and you can come back tomorrow when we're open."

"But the front door was unlocked," Susan said.

"And you have to break a few eggs to make a cake," I replied. "Both statements that have no bearing on your spectacular law-breaking." I knew since I was practically a professional at law-breaking at this point. Ironically, you really did need to break a couple of eggs to make a cake, or a few windows to solve a murder case.

"Surely, you can make an exception for me. I'm from out of town. And it's late. I'm hungry, and—"

"And there's a sign that says 'closed' in the front door." I walked to it and opened it for her.

Susan trudged out of it and onto the sidewalk, pausing in the early evening to glare at me like it would make a difference to my decision. "This is a weird town."

"The word you're looking for is 'mysterious.'" I shut the door and locked it this time then returned to the kitchen and my cake. I had a soft spot for good people, but I wouldn't tolerate those who were rude. Entering a closed bakery and demanding service was decidedly rude.

And I had so much on my plate.

The cake batter was smooth and well-mixed, and I poured it into the prepared pans, relishing the moments of silence. The soft ticking of the clock was a little less annoying than it had been a few hours ago.

I made a buttercream, a ganache thereafter, and once the cakes were done, placed them on wire racks to cool. They were as perfect as I could have wanted them to be.

Assembling the cake was like putting on clothes or brushing my teeth. It was second-nature to me at this point, and the finished product was beautiful.

A double layer cake that was soft and moist, light and airy, with a perfect sugary buttercream and a hidden ganache filling. I smiled at the cake, tears gathering in my eyes.

"Silly," I muttered, removing a handkerchief from the pocket of my apron. I dabbed at the corners of my eyes.

Heavens, in all that time, I still hadn't managed to come up with a solution to my problem. How on earth was I going to deal with Detective Mike Winters?

Mike who had taken me on several dates, each more fun and thrilling than the last. Mike who appeared to be caring and kind, and who wanted to be more than just a casual date.

My heart turned at the thought of it.

I couldn't possibly relinquish my independence. Doing that would be like betraying my Robert. I squeezed my eyes shut, remembering my husband, taken from me before I could make sense of the fact that he was gone.

I shook my head, covered the cake, then left the bakery kitchen in darkness.

Ruby had left her car at the bakery for me to use, so I slipped into the Chevrolet Cruze and started the short journey home, rolling down the windows to let in the summery salt-specked air from the bay.

Mystery wasn't *weird*. People were so fond of that word nowadays. But it wasn't weird to me. It was full of excitement and newness, even though it had been nearly a year since we had moved out here. It was the start of a chapter in my life.

But I wasn't sure how *new* I wanted that chapter to be.

I averted my thoughts toward dinner—Jamie was a fantastic cook, and I'd heard him mention gnocchi when he'd dropped by the bakery this afternoon. There was nothing better than a good plate of gnocchi or lasagna. Besides baking or solving a case.

If only there was another one of those to go around.

I drove down the winding road that led further into town, past the local cemetery and—

The car lights flashed across a forlorn figure on the side of the road. A caramel-colored dachshund huddled near the closed gates to the cemetery, its ears flat and its tail between its legs. I pulled over and got out of the car, frowning.

"Hey, puppy," I whispered, approaching it with a hand out.

It lifted one paw and shuffling backward.

"It's OK, little guy," I said. "What are you doing out here?"

The caramel dachshund wore a woven collar but no tags. He was skinny, as if he didn't have regular meals, and I gritted my teeth in anger at the thought of that. What horrible cretin would leave a defenseless animal out here?

I bent and extended a hand to the dog. "There you go. Take a sniff."

The dachshund sniffed my fingers tentatively and gave a wag of its tail.

"All right," I said, "here's the deal. You can come home with me and have something to eat, or you can stay here. Wag once if you want food."

The dog wagged its tail several times, but I took it as a "yes." I carefully approached and lifted it from the gravel path that led into the cemetery, tucking it against my chest. The dog didn't growl or snap or act afraid. It seemed grateful I had found it.

Tomorrow, I'd take it to the local vet and find out if it was microchipped. As of now, it was a stray in need of a home. "There you go. I've got news for you. There's a cat living back at the house, so you'd better get used to—"

A flash of light distracted me, and I froze.

"What on earth—?"

The flash came again, and I found the source—a beam of light in the cemetery. I peered through the iron rungs of the gates, curious. A second beam of light joined the first, and then both bobbed out of sight, as if the bearers had moved further into the cemetery and out of sight.

That was something. "The caretaker," I said to the dog. "Don't worry about him. He's got business in there that we don't want to get involved in."

The dog barked loudly in agreement, and I took him back to the Chevrolet. "Come on," I said. "You need a bath, and I need a bowl full of gnocchi."

Two

The following morning...

"If he's not microchipped, you should keep him." Leslie held a bowl of buttercream frosting, a smile playing at the corners of her lips. "A new dog in the family? That's wicked. What will you call him?"

"Dogs are big responsibilities," I said, but I smiled anyway. The dog, I had taken to calling him Caramel in my mind, was affectionate and talkative. He'd barked the house down when I'd arrived back home and both Ruby and Jamie thought keeping him would be a great idea.

This morning, I had taken a trip to the local vet and found out he wasn't microchipped, but he had a collar,

ROSIE A. POINT

and it was important I ensure I wasn't keeping someone else's dog. Even though they clearly couldn't look after Caramel properly.

The kitchen door opened, and Ruby stepped inside, still with her newlywed glow. She had taken a month-long honeymoon with Jamie after the wedding and hadn't stopped smiling since.

"Good morning," Ruby sang, ruffling her short brown hair. "What's on our specials list this week? Anything fun I should know about?"

"Devil's Food Cake," I said. "The perfect cake for summer."

"Wonderful." Ruby came over to the steel kitchen countertop, pausing to check her watch. "We've got about fifteen minutes until we open the doors. Which is just enough time to have our pre-opening chat."

"Ooh." Leslie was in the process of icing a cake, and she shot keen glances at Ruby, her dark eyes wide as if she could absorb information from Ruby without her having to speak it out loud. "What do you wanna talk about?"

"Well," Ruby said, "let's see. I'm doing an iced coffee special out there that will go down well with the Devil's Food Cake. And then there's the fact that Bee might have a new dog."

"We'll see. I'm going to talk to the local shelter and see if anyone's missing a dog first."

Ruby nodded. "And, of course, there's the fact that I spotted a certain handsome detective driving by to check if we're open a while ago. I bet he'll pay us a visit soon."

My cheeks heated, and I cursed myself mentally. I had been on plenty of dates with Mike. There was no point getting wound up about him anymore, but whenever someone mentioned it reminded me of *the problem*.

The longer I spent with Mike, the more I started to enjoy his company.

"When are you going out with him again, Bee?" Ruby asked innocently. "It's been a while hasn't it?"

"No. It's been exactly as long as it should be," I said. "Just because we've been on a couple of dates doesn't mean we're serious."

"If you say so," Ruby said, "but I'm not sure Mike has got the same message. I think, he—"

"We should open up the bakery soon."

"Bee." Ruby pursed her lips at me.

Leslie looked from me to Ruby and back again, her eyes wide with concern.

"Talking about Mike is a waste of our time. We have cakes to bake."

Ruby patted me on the shoulder gently. "You're going to have to learn to let go eventually, Bee. No woman is an island."

"Depends on what you believe."

Ruby dropped the topic and exited the kitchen, leaving Leslie and me to finish up the Devil's Food Cake. The sooner we got into the swing of things, the better. I was happy at the thought of a new pet, especially an adorable dachshund like Caramel. The dog had been intrigued by Cookie, who had treated him with a haughty disdain.

On occasion, I'd imagine I heard Cookie's thoughts, and last night, they'd all been centered around her superiority to this new "butt-licker" who'd entered his home. The irony being that Cookie had a penchant for washing his derriere.

I took the cake from the countertop and entered the dining room, my gaze on the refrigerated cake stand where it would be kept for the day. The bakery bustled with the hubbub of gathered customers, a few lined up in front of the counter to be served by Ruby, others already seated and being tended to by our server, Farrah.

"—believe it! And right at the start of the tourist season too." The voice of a customer carried through the interior of the bakery.

"It's a curse," a man said. "Mystery is cursed thanks to this. Tourist season's going to be mighty dry."

I tucked the cake into the glass case refrigerator then turned, frowning at the two having the conversation. Both were familiar—Joseph from the butchery and Haley from the library, good friends who often stopped by for a slice of cake and a coffee in the morning.

Something about their tone had sent that quiver of intrigue up my spine and into my mind. Anything that might affect the tourist season was important. We needed all the customers we could get this summer. Business could be better—we were new to town, and I wanted the bakery to be a raging success.

"What are you two talking about?" I walked over to them.

"Mornin', Bee," Joseph said, adjusting his belt. He was a no frills man, peach fuzz on his head, and a stare that went through a person rather than focusing on them.

"You haven't heard." Haley pressed her glasses up the bridge of her nose and they slid down to the tip once again. Short and costumed in jewels and a kaftan-dress creation, she reminded me of a cake that had been decorated by a toddler. But she was nice—as nice as most people were when they weren't murdering others.

"Enlighten me," I said. "What's happening?"

"They found *three* bodies this morning." Joseph put up the corresponding number of stubby fingers. "Three."

"Bodies," I said. "Corpses?"

"Ayuh."

"Where? How?"

"Some rig went and dug 'em up in the cemetery last night," Joseph said.

Haley shuddered. "It gives me the creeps, thinking about it. People out there digging up the dead."

"It's a curse," Joseph said. "Digging up people's corpses like that? A curse, I tell ya. And we're going to pay the price for it here. This will drive off all the flatlanders. Much as I hate to say it, we need the money they bring in. Old Carol at the Milkweed's going to have a cat, two dogs, and a cow when she finds out about this. You know how she makes most of her money during the summer."

I kept my expression calm. Last night, I'd seen the lights inside the cemetery. Flashlights. My assumption had been that the caretaker was doing his job, but now, the memory had a different connotation. Grave robbers. Here. In Mystery?

Caramel must belong to one of them.

Why else would the dog have been on the side of the road, shivering in fear?

"Any idea who they are?" I asked. "The bodies?"

Haley shook her head, pale all over. "No, but I hear a lot of folks are going down to the cemetery this morning to find out what happened."

"It's not right," Joseph said. "The place is meant to be locked 'cept during visiting hours. The caretaker's to blame for this."

"What's going on?" Ruby asked.

It was then I realized the entire bakery had been listening in on our conversation. I tapped my chin. "Hmm."

"Bee?"

"They found three bodies this mornin'," Joseph said, launching into the tale. "Three graves dug up. The gates to the cemetery open. And the bodies were left out on the grass."

Ruby pressed a hand over her mouth. "That's horrifying."

"So horrifying I have to see it for myself," I said.

"Bee?"

"Do you want to come with me?" I asked her, in case this was too much for her stomach to handle.

She gnawed her lip but there was a light in her eyes that I recognized. She was intrigued, even through her horror at what had happened.

"That's what I thought," I said. "You tell Farrah, I'll tell Leslie. Let's find out what's going on in our town."

Three

THERE WASN'T A SHOT IN ALL THAT WAS HOT AND fiery that I'd let this case get away from me. Three bodies and a grave robber added up to a plot of some type, and I was going to figure out what it meant. Before the police did. Every case I solved brought me one step closer to the truth. To proving that I didn't need anyone to protect me or—

"It's so busy!" Ruby parked her Chevrolet Cruze on the side of the road behind another car and stared, jaw dropped, at the front of the cemetery.

She wasn't wrong. The front gates of the cemetery were barely visible thanks to the throng of onlookers. Police vehicles were parked up and down the road, and a yellow line had been put up to force people back.

A rather irritable looking office was positioned near

the front of the crowd, the top of his head visible and creased with frown lines.

"Looks like everybody wants answers."

"But it might not be anything serious. Maybe we shouldn't bother that poor officer."

I got out of the car and hurried across the street, unable to contain my curiosity. I forced my way through the crowd, Ruby joining me a moment later, and we reached the front of the group to find Officer Abbott, fists on his hips.

"You stay back now," he said to the group of people. "You're all angry, I get it, but you can't shoot the darn messenger. It's the mayor you'll want to talk to."

"Where is he?" A man cried, and I turned to find it was Joseph who had spoken, Haley right next to him. Both were pink-cheeked, swept up in the anger that surrounded them.

Crowds were like that—it was easy to get riled up once you were in a group. Massive crowds turned the most intellectual woman into a pack animal if the atmosphere was right.

"He'll be along when he's along," Officer Abbott said, putting out his thick-fingered hands. He'd come into the bakery a few times and had selected lemon curd filled donuts for his brunch. An interesting choice that indicated he was both kind and prone to anger. You could tell a lot about a person by the sweets they ate.

"You've gotta give us more than that, Rodney," Haley said. "People deserve answers. They've got stores and restaurants to run. Bakeries. We're putting on a summer show for the kids at the library. You can't just—"

"That's enough," Abbott grunted. "I can't tell you what I don't know." And then he took a step behind the line and stood there with his cellphone out, gazing at the screen rather than the crowd.

I scanned the movement inside the cemetery, curiously. The police moved back and forth, tents and screens up to guard the public from viewing what was going on inside.

"Mike must be in there," I murmured to Ruby.

As the town detective, Mike didn't just investigate murders. Major thefts or crimes that needed investigative work were part of his job description, especially since Mystery's police department serviced the entire county and the smaller towns within it who didn't have their own station.

"Do you think it was murder?" Ruby asked. "It can't be, though. Right? They were just bodies that were dug up. Maybe they were trying to steal things from them?"

"Hmm." I tapped my chin. "We need to know who was exhumed."

"Can you call it an exhumation in this case?" Ruby

shifted her weight from one foot to the other. "I can't believe this has happened. Why would anyone want to dig up people's graves?"

"Jewelry," I said.

"Jewelry? But, it's not like these people were Egyptian mummies or something. They're regular people."

Which brought me back to my initial question. Who were the people who'd been dug up so unceremoniously?

I tapped Haley on the shoulder, and she turned toward me, her kaftan-dress floating in the breeze. "The mayor better get his lard butt down here before—"

"Who were they, Haley?"

"Huh?"

"The people who were..." I mimed digging.

Ruby let out a horrified noise beside me.

"Oh. I think Joseph knows now," Haley said, and tugged on her friend's arm. "You know who they were, Jo? The folks who were, you know—?"

"Oh, right, see, that's the interesting part," Joseph said, leaning around the librarian to make eye contact with me. "There were three of 'em, right? First, somebody was dug up from the unmarked grave."

"The unmarked grave?" Ruby asked.

"Ayuh. Only one of 'em in the entire cemetery. Nobody knows who was buried there, but it was in and around the sixties when it popped up. Or so they say. I was still a boy, and it was all the news at the time, you know. I remember hot summer nights when we'd come out to the cemetery and try sneaking in to see the gravestone. Of course, Tenny the old caretaker would always catch us and chase us out before we got close. Never forget the rush though. And the smell of the—"

"Who else, Jo?" Haley tapped her heel on the sidewalk. An impatient woman after my own heart.

"All right, darn. Keep your kaftan on," he said. "Anyway, the first was the unmarked grave. Then there was a grave that's been damaged. Can't even read the gravestone, so I have no idea who it was, and the last one... Now, that's real interesting."

"Why?" I asked.

"'Cos the last grave that got dug up was... well, it was Connie Gardener's," Jo said, raising his eyebrows so high it made him seem like an egg with eyebrows drawn on.

Haley gasped, bracelets clattering as her hand flew to her cover her lips.

"Who's Connie Gardener, Jo?" Ruby asked delicately.

"Connie was a wonderful girl," he said. "Also died when I was a boy. She was a teacher at the Mystery kindergarten. And she was murdered. Cops never solved her case."

Now, he had my attention. Someone had dug up the

grave of a murder victim? "Connie Gardener," I said. "Does she have any—"

Officer Abbott let out a rough whistle, his hand on the radio attached to his uniformed shoulder.

The crowd quieted.

"You can go back to your homes," he said. "Mayor Miller's called an emergency meeting in the town hall tonight at 08:00 p.m. sharp. You can ask him your questions then."

A grumble rushed through the crowd, the news spreading and discussed, torn apart and put back together again by the town residents. People wanted answers.

I caught a glimpse of Mike moving inside the cemetery between the stones, and my heart skipped a beat. I turned away, meeting Ruby's gaze. "Want to go to a town meeting?"

She nodded.

Four

I WASN'T PRONE TO ANXIETY, BUT EVER SINCE THE three bodies had appeared, a ball of iron had formed in the pit of my stomach and wouldn't budge. Three bodies. And one of them belonged to the victim of a cold case that had never been solved. That was too interesting to pass up, so why was I so nervous.

Ruby and I filed into the town hall—open to the public only when the council and mayor deemed it necessary—and took seats on plastic chairs near the back of the room. Sitting in the back served two purposes. First, we could easily hide from prying eyes, and second, we could study everyone's reactions to whatever the mayor had to say.

The Mystery Town Hall wasn't particularly grand, but

it had a raised stage and a microphone with a stand for meetings like this one.

Ruby shifted on her chair beside me and the plastic made a squeak. "These chairs are hard," she whispered. "I'm going to need to see a chiropractor after this."

"This sounds like a privileged rich woman problem," I whispered back.

Ruby blushed, but I patted her on the arm to let her know I was kidding. My nerves were getting to me. Ruby was the last person I wanted to lash out at during times of stress.

The town hall filled up fast with faces we recognized and a few we didn't. Haley and Joseph sat together near the front, and Betty, the mayor's wife, had taken up a position near the front as well. She kept glancing around, her usually happy face pulled into a scowl. The last event she'd run had ended before it had had a chance to begin, so I could understand her frustration. Nobody wanted the tourist season to end early this year.

Ruby nudged me and wriggled her eyebrows at the side door near the stage.

Mike, the town detective, stood there, talking to someone out of sight. My heart turned over, and I let out a slow breath. Of course, the man had chosen to look incredibly handsome this evening. He wore a plain buttoned shirt, with a pair of jeans, a lanyard hanging around his neck, and his salt and pepper beard groomed neatly.

"This is serious, isn't it?" Ruby whispered behind her hand. "I mean, I know it's three dead bodies, but if Mike is talking to the mayor..."

Mayor Miller, a thin man who walked with a limp and had keen, brown eyes, strode up the side steps of the stage, escorted by Mike. He stopped in front of the microphone, and the noise in the hall dulled.

"Good evening, everyone," Mayor Miller said, voice deep and smooth. "Thank you for convening on short notice."

"What's goin' on?" A man in the front row stood up, raising his hand. "We deserve to know what's happening in *our* town, 'specially during tourist season."

"Take a seat, Ned," Mike said. "Let the mayor finish what he's got to say before you start askin' questions."

Ned grumbled and sat back down, folding his arms. I had a vague memory of him—the new owner of the gun store?

"Now, I know you're all worried about what's happened," Mayor Miller said, enunciating his words loudly and clearly into the microphone. "But yelling about it isn't going to help anyone. Let me finish, and you can ask your questions at the end. All right?"

A grumble of assent went through the crowd. I

scanned the people gathered, the sides of faces, the intent expressions. Most of these people were business owners, and there was tension in the air.

"This morning, Officer Abbott of the Mystery Police Department responded to a report of three dead bodies in the Mystery Cemetery," Mayor Miller said. "The bodies of three of our citizens were dug up. Detective Winters here has got more details."

Mike stepped up to talk, and that ball of iron tripled in size.

"Evenin' folks," he said. "As the mayor said, this morning, three bodies were recovered from the Mystery Cemetery. They were dug up by what looks to be grave robbers. Given recent events, we thought it would be a good idea to inform you that there have not been any new murders in Mystery."

Several people let out relieved sighs.

"But who dug them up?" Someone cried out.

"Questions at the end, Mr. Tolbart," Mayor Miller said, from the back of the stage.

"Hard tellin', not knowin'," Mike said, in his gruff, throaty growl. "But rest assure that the Mystery police are doing everything we can to find out who did this. Right now, it's lookin' like a simple case of grave robbing. There's no need to be alarmed, but if you have any information that could lead to an arrest, report it." He stepped aside.

Mayor Miller returned to the microphone and adjusted it, eliciting a few *bops* of noise. "That's all there is to know, folks," he said. "Summer's going to be great this year. Just keep calm and everything will go according to plan. I'll open it up to questions now."

Several hands shot into the air, and I leaned forward, studying the tension-lined faces. It didn't matter what Mike or the mayor said. People were sure this was going to end badly. And I was too—it didn't make sense that someone would go through all this effort just to dig up three bodies. It wasn't like these people were pharaohs hiding gold and riches in their graves. Something fishy was going on.

"—hide this from people from away?" That had come from Penny, who ran a local antique store. In every small town we'd ever visited, there were an abundance of antique stores. Mystery was no exception.

"There's nothing to hide," Mayor Miller said, a little irritably. "It's just a case of petty theft."

"But grave robbing is messing around with a dead body," Penny said, not to be deterred. "Ain't that a felony? And what if the paper runs a piece on what happened? Anyone who sees it will know about it and—"

"We're in talks with the editor or the paper," Mayor Miller said.

"In talks?" Penny wasn't to be deterred.

"That's all the questions I'll take," Mayor Miller said. "Good evening, everyone. Go home and rest. There's no reason to worry."

I turned to Ruby, shaking my head. "There's more to this than meets the eye, Rubes."

My friend bit on the corner of her lip which was her anxiety tell—she wasn't sure whether she wanted to get involved or not. Thankfully, I'd already made that decision for the both of us.

Five

Later that evening...

"FANTASTIC AS USUAL, JAMIE," I SAID, FINISHING off the last bite of a Mediterranean chicken salad he'd made for us tonight. Jamie had opted to make summer salads more often of late, and I'd thought I wouldn't like them after the fantastic lobster lasagnas and soups he'd made during winter. I'd been wrong.

Ruby sat back, Cookie, our pet ginger cat in her lap, and smiled happily. "The more you cook for us, the more convinced I am that you should be a chef rather than an author."

"I could easily take offense to that," Jamie said, sending

her a special smile. "But I know you mean that in a nice way."

Ruby let out a fantastic yawn, and I did the same. It wasn't particularly late, but it was past my bedtime for a day that had been filled with "excitement" and nerves. I glanced over at the corner of the room, where the gorgeous golden dachshund lay sleeping, its snout resting on its paws.

"I'd better get back to the cottage. Look how tired poor little Caramel is." I rose from the table. "Oh, wait, you need help with the dishes."

"No, no," Jamie said. "I've got this. I enjoy doing them. It's therapeutic."

"You sure lucked out, Ruby." I grinned at my friend.

"I'm sure Mike would do your dishes if you asked him to," Ruby said.

My smile faded right away. "I'd better get home."

"Bee."

"Thanks for the meal. Have a great rest of your night, you two." I collected the sleeping stray dog from the corner, and the dachshund let out a whine and snuggled deeper into my arms.

I brought the dog out into the night, shutting the front door behind me, and stood on the front porch, breathing in the soft scents of the distant ocean, the blooming flowers in the garden, and the familiar earthy smell of coming rain.

I stroked Caramel's head. The dog didn't have a home —it was official. He wasn't chipped, and a quick visit to the local shelter had revealed that nobody had come by looking for him. I'd left my details just in case, but the general consensus was that if nobody dropped in within the week, Caramel was a stray.

And in that case, I could choose to keep him.

"You're too cute for your own good," I whispered to Caramel, stroking his velvety soft ears.

He wagged his tail against my arms.

I sighed and walked down the porch stairs, circling the house beneath the moonlight. Jamie had decorated the long path toward my cottage at the back of their property with solar lanterns. Honestly, the walk home every evening was idyllic, but I was in a strange mood tonight.

Three corpses.

And being interested in the town detective. Of course, there was the fact that this gorgeous dog in my arms could belong to the same person who had dug up those graves. In that case, I was all for keeping Caramel—he deserved better than being a look out for a criminal.

I unlocked my cottage door and let myself in.

As always, my little home smelled like lavender and baked cookies—two of my favorite scents. I had a bedroom off to one side with a double bed, a small bathroom, an open plan living room and kitchen, the living area decorated with a leather loveseat, a coffee table, tiny bookcase and a TV. It was all I had ever wanted or needed.

I put Caramel down on the sofa, ensured that his water and food bowls were full, then went through to my closet in the bedroom.

I didn't need to click on the light to find what I was looking for. A shoebox on the top shelf. I brought it down, returned to the living room, and sat down.

"I'm not sure about this, Caramel," I said. "And it takes a lot for me to say that." I made it my business to be sure of things. And to tackle things head on too. If my beloved grandmother had taught me anything, besides fishing and baking, it was that facing one's fears head-on was the only way to make them go away. Avoiding things didn't help. Hiding from problems was for weak people. Her words.

I opened the shoebox and brought out the pictures.

There were many, but I focused on the first three.

The first was from the day I'd met Robert. We were both young, me wearing that ridiculously tight pair of bell bottom jeans—whoever thought those were a great idea? I had a flower in my hair, which was long and blonde, and stood with my hands pressed together in front of me, side-by-side with Robert. We were sixteen.

Robert was exactly as I remembered. His dark hair out of control and flyaway, his eyebrows bushy and his eyes kind and so full of life.

My throat closed, and I pressed a hand over it, forcing myself to exhale.

The next image was of our wedding. I wore my grandmother's dress, long, and lacy, high-necked and long-sleeved. Robert had opted for his police uniform. It was before he'd taken his detective's test. He was dapper, his hair combed appropriately, and his gaze resting on me.

I remembered that night like it was yesterday—if I closed my eyes, I could smell his cologne, I could see his smile as he whirled me around on the dance floor.

Tears streamed down my cheeks as I brought out the final picture. One most recent, when we'd been in our forties, older and wiser—or so I'd thought, ha—at our dinner table with friends. A week before Robert had been murdered.

I dropped the pictures back into the shoebox and closed it, holding it to my body.

Caramel got up and sat beside me, pressing his warm dog body against mine. He let out a soft sigh, and I stroked him, taking comfort from his presence and fur.

"What would he have wanted me to do?" I asked. "He would want me to figure out what happened. He would want me to be independent. He would want—"

My phone buzzed on the coffee table, and I spied the screen. Mike's name flashed on it, and I shut my eyes, letting it go to voicemail.

Tomorrow, I'd tackle everything head on, like my grandmother would have wanted. Like Robert would expect. If I couldn't solve his case, then I'd solve darn near every other one that crossed my path. Without anyone's help.

Six

"ARE YOU SURE ABOUT THIS, BEE?" RUBY ASKED. "I'm sure that Mike has everything under control. You heard what the mayor said last night, right?"

"What the mayor said and what Mike's doing is none of our concern," I said. "People are unhappy, Ruby. Look at them." I stood just outside the doorway to the kitchen, surveying the interior of the bakery with a critical eye.

The customers filled the tables, and many of them wore those same tense expressions as the townsfolk in the hall last night. People weren't convinced that the mayor and local law enforcement had this under control. And neither was I.

Mike might have it somewhat under control, but I know we can figure this out.

"It's not even like there was a murder," Ruby said.

"There's a cold case. Surely, you're intrigued about that."

She gave an infinitesimal nod.

"I'll take that as a yes," I said. "Regardless, I'm going."

"You're going? Going where?"

"To the cemetery," I said.

"Oh, Bee, keep your voice down. People will hear you."

And she was right. A few of the nearby customers had looked up at the mention of the cemetery, but that was just because everyone was on edge about it. I didn't care either way. The minute there was a lull in activity, I'd leave.

"The morning rush is almost over," I said. "Are you coming with me or not?"

Ruby gnawed on her lip. "Yeah. I guess it won't hurt to find out what happened at the cemetery, especially after what you saw."

The flashlights in the cemetery the night before. I hadn't told Mike about that yet. I wanted to find out what was going on for myself first. I left Ruby to tend to the customers and entered the kitchen. Leslie was making another Devil's Food Cake—we'd been selling out of slices like crazy. As expected, summer was the time for Devil's Food Cake, probably because of all the evil at work in Mystery at the moment.

Heat always brought out the worst in people.

I helped Leslie with the frosting then exited into the bakery after a half an hour. Thankfully, it had quieted down. I gestured for Ruby to follow me, then headed out of the front door and into the street. It was a typical, busy day in Mystery, and our bakery had a lovely view of the bay.

The waters were smooth, and there were plenty of people down on the beach, enjoying the start of summer. The lobster boats had already left, though there weren't that many of them in Mystery, and the other restaurants that bordered the bay hummed with activity.

"Looks like the news hasn't deterred anybody," I muttered.

"I don't know about that. Apparently, *the Mystery Mail* is going to run a feature on what happened."

"Hmm." I scratched my chin. "So much for Mayor Miller getting the editor of the paper to hold off on that. I bet Penny's in an uproar over this."

Ruby let out a sigh. "Probably. Oh, this is terrible, Bee. I wish things would settle down around here. Just when we were finally getting everything back on track after that whole baking contest debauchery, this happens."

"Don't worry too much," I said. "We've got this under control."

But Ruby let out another breath that didn't exactly instill confidence in our investigating skills. We got into her navy blue car and took the winding drive over to the cemetery with the windows down and the scent of salty ocean air drifting in.

I was glad we'd chosen a place by the ocean. The beach towns we'd visited on our travels in the food truck had always been my favorite, although that salt air did a number on my hair. Always made it feel ... fudgey.

"We're here." Ruby parked the car outside the cemetery.

The police line was still up across the gates, but a single guard sat out front on a chair wearing blue overalls and a nametag. He wasn't with the police.

I marched over to him the minute Ruby cut the engine.

The guy was half-asleep, his heavy eyelids drooping over eyes that were too big for his face. His chair leaned against the stone column next to the gate, right below a bronze plaque that read **Mystery Cemetery** in sweeping letters. His nametag identified him as Nate, and underneath that, his title read, *Mystery Cemetery Caretaker.* He breathed evenly and gave a snore.

Great security guard.

Ruby rushed up to join me, a look of urgency on her face.

I lifted a foot, placed it on the bottom rung of the

chair, and tipped it forward so that it landed on four legs with an unceremonious thump.

Nate gasp-snorted and shocked away, throwing out his hands. "Warner, you dubbah, I'll—" He blinked those too big green eyes at us. "Who—? Where? What are you doing here?" And then he shook his head, allegedly coming to what little senses he had left. "You cannot pass."

"All right, Gandalf," I said. "We don't want to pass."

"Ganda...?" Nate blinked. "Huh? Look, this cemetery's off-limits. Nobody goes in and nobody comes out. Them's the rules, lady."

"Good morning, Nate," Ruby said, in her polite, "I'm about to charm you so you tell me what I want" tone. "We were just here to find out what happened. We heard the news that people were—"

"I look like a cop to you?" Nate snorted. "I don't know nothing about nothing, OK? I'm just here to make sure nobody goes in, and nobody comes out."

"The nobody goes in part I get," I said. "But who are you expecting to come out? The walking dead?"

Nate smacked his lips a couple of times, searching for an answer to my question in the dry and dusty annals of his mind. "You were the one who tipped my chair forward, weren't ya?" He pointed at me.

So he'd chosen to divert instead. "Are you the usual caretaker of this place?"

"Sure, I am," he said, sitting straighter, a hint of pride entering his tone. "It's a family job, see? My dad, Tenny, did this before me, and his dad, George, did it before him. Nothing happens in this cemetery that I don't know about."

"It stands to reason that you know what happened here on the night that the graves were tampered with then," I said expectantly.

"I don't know nothing about that."

"But you just said that you know everything that happens here."

"Look, lady, I'm just the caretaker. I do my job, and I make sure the place is looking good for the people who want to visit their deceased loved ones," he said. "I—"

"I'm sure the visitors to this cemetery are happy with the job you've done so far, what with the mounds of dirt and corpses lying around," I said irritably.

"Bee." Ruby squeezed my arm. "What she means is that the people in town are worried about what happened here. We're just wondering if you might have seen something. After all, you are the guy who knows everything about this place." She smiled sweetly at him.

Nate sniffed, wriggled his nose, then spat off to one side. "Wish I could help," he said. "But if you want to know what's going on, you should talk to the police. Or, you know, ask your husbands. They probably know more about it than you do."

"What on earth is *that* supposed to mean?" I bristled.

He shrugged. "The men in this town know what's what is all I'm saying." And then he leaned back in his chair again, and shut his eyes, arms folded across his scrawning chest.

I envisioned throwing a milkshake at him. It was part of my "red light, yellow light, green light" anger management process. If I stopped and pictured exacting my revenge or anger, I was less likely to act it out in real life. It was much easier to stop myself when I'd seen a mental image of how silly I looked lobbing food or drinks. And there was the mental satisfaction of having done it too.

I opened my mouth to lecture the young whippersnapper, but Ruby squeezed my arm a second time, and I let it go. For now.

The security guard was officially my prime suspect.

Seven

LATER THAT EVENING, AFTER WE'D CLOSED THE doors to the bakery and seen the last of the customers off, Leslie, Ruby, and I sat down at our favorite table in the bakery. I took a moment to admire the interior of our little home away from home. The walls were decorated in murals with cartoonish images of bees and honeycombs, and the bakery was possessed of a coziness even in the summer months, that brought me happiness.

In times like these, I still couldn't believe that I had a bakery of my own. My grandmother would've been so proud.

It was our custom to finish off the day with a cup of hot chocolate or, in the summer, iced tea or lemonade, with cupcakes or cookies or donuts. I had to go easy on the sugar at night or I wouldn't sleep, but it was my favorite way to end the day.

Particularly when there was a murder for us to solve or a mystery in this case. Though, there was that cold case which technically counted as a murder, didn't it?

"What a day," Ruby said, placing a tray with drinks and slices of cake in the center of the table. I helped myself to one.

We had cut up the Devil's Food Cake as a treat for this evening's gossip session.

"I can't believe it," Leslie said. "Mystery's been so strange lately. There were the murders and now this. Three whole bodies dug up in the cemetery. It's no wonder people are in a bad mood."

"Three whole bodies," I said, "as opposed to three dismemb—"

"Oh, Bee, don't!" Ruby put a hand over her stomach. "I won't enjoy this cake if you say something like that."

"Sorry. Bad joke."

Leslie took a bite of her cake and closed her eyes, a smile on her lips. "I'll never get tired of working here. The cakes. The company."

"The mysteries to solve," I prompted.

Ruby gave me a long-suffering look. She knew I wasn't going to let this one go. Was it me, or was Ruby more adverse to investigating crimes now that she was married?

She'd truly settled down. I was happy for her, but no amount of settling would keep me from sleuthing.

"Have you thought about it?" Leslie asked. "Y'know, the crime? I heard from Wendy at SumFruit that the police are real worried about it."

"They are?" Ruby asked.

"Ayuh. After what happened the last couple of months, they should be. They're talking about a crime trend. First murders, and now this. Wendy said she heard Old Carol complaining about the town going to heck, and how the flatlanders wouldn't be interested in our town anymore."

"Hmm." I tapped my chin.

There had to be extra pressure on the police department to perform. I hadn't talked to Mike yet today, but he'd left me a message asking to chat over coffee some time. And I wasn't going to have a heart-skipping moment over that.

"Old Carol said she was going to put in a formal complaint with the police. And the paper is running a feature, so that can't be good." Leslie cut off a piece of cake with the side of her fork and lifted it. "I heard that the cops are thinking of bringing in outside help."

"Outside help?"

"That's the rumor," Leslie said. "But it could be wrong."

It made sense, but it would also upset Mike if they brought in outside help. He was passionate about his job, and he wouldn't like anyone interfering any more than I did.

"We went to talk to the caretaker of the cemetery today," Ruby said. "Nate?"

"Tenny's son." Leslie nodded. "Laziest man I've ever had the displeasure of making acquaintance with. He'd happily do anything to avoid a day of hard work."

"That was the impression we got," I said. "He was asleep when we got there."

"You wanted to know more about what happened." Leslie's eyes lit up. She loved it when we investigated crimes—lived through us vicariously. She had a family to care for, so she preferred not to get involved.

What would that have been like? Having a family. Robert and I had come close a few times.

I've been thinking about him a lot more than usual.

My husband was often in my thoughts, but I had slowly moved forward after his death. These days, it felt like a regression back into grief and sorrow. I'd thought I'd dealt with most of my emotions over losing him.

"Do you think Nate had anything to do with it?" Ruby asked.

"With those graves being dug up?" Leslie considered it for a moment, taking a sip of ice tea, the cubes clinking against the glass. "I don't know. Nate's lazy but he's not malicious. And I don't see why he would want to do that. I don't see why anyone would want to do that." She shivered.

I had the same opinion. This was fishy. Why would anyone want to dig up the deceased? There were no motiveless crimes, so there had to be a reason.

It could have something to do with the cold case.

That was a lead I would love to investigate. A cold case was a challenge, depending on how it had gone down. If the police hadn't bothered investigating it properly or—

"Nate isn't a bad guy," Leslie said, "but he was the only caretaker at the Mystery Cemetery. And the only one who has the keys to the gates."

"When I drove past there the night before, the gates were closed," I said, "but I'm not sure if they were locked. And there were multiple flashlights moving around inside."

Leslie gasped. "You told Detective Winters about this?"

"Not yet," I said.

Ruby gave me a look.

"I will. I'll tell him. But first, I'd like to—"

A sharp knock came at the bakery door. This was my pet peeve—people knocking on the door when the sign in the glass clearly read "CLOSED" in big, bold letters.

I turned to gesture to the person to go away, but stopped at the sight of the man standing there.

He was young, with a bulbous nose, and he wore a striped shirt. He reminded me of an oversized candy cane, slightly leaning to one side. Most importantly, a lanyard with identification hung around his neck.

The man was a detective. And he was most definitely not *my* detective.

"Oh no," Ruby breathed.

There was that old adage about not reading books by their covers, but who stuck to that anymore? Nobody.

I got up and let in the newcomer.

"Good evening, ladies," he said. "Allow me to introduce myself. I'm Detective Rourke. Come down from Portland to help out around here."

"I'm Ruby, this is Bee, and that's Leslie." My friend was always willing to make the introductions while my questions burned a hole in my brain.

"What are you doing here?" I asked.

"Heard a rumor, whisper in the leaves, that you two are good at solving crimes," Detective Rourke said, casting those beady eyes from side-to-side to take both Ruby and me in. "I wanted to drop by and tell you to keep your eyes, ears, fingers, and everything else away from my case. I run a strict no interference policy. You mess with that policy, you answer to me." And then he nodded to us and walked for the door.

"Hey," I called out. "Where's Mike?"

"Detective Winters is back at the precinct, waiting for my help." Rourke smirked at me before exiting into the night.

If I'd been sure I was going to figure out what happened, I was more determined now.

Eight

Later that night...

I SAT ON MY LITTLE SOFA IN THE COTTAGE, A MUG of hot chocolate on the coffee table, and my laptop on my lap. Caramel had curled up beside me after a yummy meal of shredded chicken breast and some water.

He was a well-behaved dog with a sweet personality, and he definitely enjoyed food as much as I did.

Occasionally, I reached over to pet him, and he would wag his tail or lick his doggy lips and yawn.

"It's been a long day," I said. "Look at the time." I adjusted my reading glasses on the tip of my nose—I hadn't needed any for years, but now things were getting a little more difficult and annoying.

The time on my laptop screen read 00:00, and that was way past my bedtime, even though I was more of a night owl than Ruby.

But I had tried sleeping, and all that had resulted in was a great deal of tossing and turning and heat creation which only irritated me more.

That Detective Rourke had a nerve. He had a need for a milkshake to the face.

I shut my eyes and went to my happy place to calm down—namely, throwing said milkshake in the detective's face.

Finally, I squared my jaw and opened the browser on my laptop.

I had a theory about Detective Rourke's appearance in town. Sure, the police might need extra help after the recent spate of murders—*pssh*, these people didn't know what a real spate of murders looked like—but why ask for help now?

Why, after a few graves had been dug up? Sure that was bad, and definitely illegal, but it wasn't like there had been multiple murders.

My theory was that the person who had dug up those bodies had done so because they wanted to find out something about the cold case. Or hide something.

And if the cold case was the reason for this, then it deserved my attention.

I didn't have much to go on apart from the victim's name. I typed it into the browser and hit return.

Results about the case popped up immediately—articles that dated back many years and even an in-depth look at what had happened by one of those true crime enthusiasts.

I clicked on it and my eyebrows lifted when I realized that this wasn't an article at all. It was a video.

A gorgeous young woman, done up in makeup, appeared on the screen. "Hello, everybody, and thank you so much for joining me for another episode of true crime cold cases. If you haven't been here before, allow me to introduce myself. My name is Ella-Mae, and I am your WatchMe crime enthusiast."

"WatchMe?" I scanned the browser bar. "Oh." It was the name of the video hosting site.

Ella-Mae continued talking, her smile bright and endearing. "I want to say thank you to our sponsor for today's episode. You can click the link in the comment box below to find out more about the exclusive offer from Rent-A-Bed. Rent-A-Bed will—"

I skipped ahead in the video using my arrow keys.

"—case today that took place way back in the sixties."

"Way back," I grunted. "What am I, chopped liver?

"Now, this is a particularly interesting case, not only because it's never been solved, but because of the way in which everything went down." Ella-Mae paused for effect. "You'll see what I mean by that in just a second. But let's start at the beginning. Connie Gardener was born on December 7, 1943, in Portland, Maine. Daughter to a wealthy doctor, Maureen, and an archaeologist and adventurer, Keith, she had a charmed childhood until, at the age of six-years-old, she was kidnapped."

I gasped. Surely, I had the wrong case here.

"Now, fortunately, Connie was found safely just two days after her abduction. It turned out that a neighbor had lured her into their house with promises of cookies and had been planning on ransoming her off to her parents because they were rich. The woman, Carlotta Dean, was arrested and later convicted for kidnapping and is still in prison to this day."

"Naturally," I said.

This was kind of fun. I liked listening to this girl talk about the crime, and it felt almost like I had a friend. Or like she was taking me on a journey.

"Of course, parents Maureen and Keith were absolutely horrified and traumatized after this happened, and they decided that living in the city was too risky, and that they needed to move to a small town where it would be safer for them and for their daughter. They chose the town of Mystery, Maine. Funny name, I know." Ella-Mae gave an adorable eye roll. "And that was truly when the real mystery began. Not long after moving, Maureen fell pregnant with another baby girl, and they welcomed Rebecca into their family. Now, Connie and Rebecca were quite a few years apart, so Connie was almost maternal toward her younger sister. It's been said that she was like a second mother to Rebecca, and the girls had a real bond."

I felt like I needed to get popcorn for this. I was getting my information delivered to me directly, and I could work with it from here. This was great.

"The girls had a, thankfully, uneventful childhood in Mystery, and attended the local schools, making friends and going through life as you do," Ella-Mae said. "Connie, for her part, was bubbly, outgoing, sweet and caring. And made friends really easily. Maureen and Keith would say that they could barely keep track of all the friends Connie kept, and that there were always kids in and out of their house."

"So, a lot of potential suspects then," I said. "But if everyone liked her..."

"In her senior year of high school, Connie met another new friend, Colton Moore. He was just as popular as she was, though he was considered as being from 'the wrong side of the tracks.'" Ella-Mae used inverted fingers. "But Connie didn't care about that, and Colton was handsome, a diligent student with a bright future, who wanted to be a part of the military when he left school. The first signs of trouble in their relationship came during the summer of 1964."

I stroked Caramel, absolutely enthralled by the story.

"It was on June 18th, when Maureen stopped outside her daughter's bedroom door to check on her and say good night. She heard the sound of crying from inside, and she knew that something was wrong. But when Maureen asked her daughter if everything was OK, Connie said that it was just a silly disagreement with Colton." Ella-Mae pulled a knowing face. "Over the next few weeks, things got progressively worse. Colton and Connie appeared to be fighting a lot, but her parents weren't too concerned. They figured that Connie would work it out with Colton —who they thought was great for her because of how diligent and focused he was. Until, that is, the morning of July 3rd, 1967. That was when everything took a horrible turn."

Nine

The following morning...

RUBY AND I SAT IN THE OFFICE AT THE BAKERY together, both watching the screen as Ella-Mae unraveled the events surrounding Connie's cold case.

"Where did you find this video?" Ruby asked. "She's really good."

"Shush, shush, she's getting to the good part," I said excitedly. If I'd thought researching the case before bed last night would help me sleep, I'd made a critical mistake. I'd spent most of this morning yawning and grumpy, apart from when I was eating donuts or trying to convince Ruby to take a break and watch this video with me.

On the screen, Ella-Mae had just reached the part where things were about to take a horrible turn.

"On the morning of July 3rd, Maureen and Keith got up and got ready for their day as they would on any other. They were popular citizens in Mystery, with Maureen the head of a local baking club, and Keith an investor in the local museum," Ella-Mae said. "It was the day after Connie's twenty-first birthday, and Maureen was keen to get the house back in shape and talk to her daughter. After all, just the day before, Maureen and Keith had gifted their daughter two expensive items. One was a custom ring, encrusted with diamonds that Keith had specially made for his daughter. Rumor had it the ring was incredibly valuable and may have been "secret". Whatever that means —I did my research and nobody seems to know. The other gift was a new car—a Ford Mustang. Both Keith and Maureen were excited for their daughter to take a ride in the new car, and they discussed it that morning, and fully expected to find Connie downstairs eating breakfast, waiting to go on a joy ride."

Ruby and I exchanged a glance. I'd already watched the full video last night, but this was just as exciting as it had been the first time around.

"But when Maureen and Keith got downstairs, they noticed that not only was Connie not downstairs eating breakfast, but her bedroom door was closed. Maureen first thought she might be sleeping in, but when she opened the door to check, Connie wasn't in her bed. In fact, the bed was a mess as if her daughter had gotten up in a hurry."

"Oh no," Ruby whispered. "Where is she?"

"That's the question." I nodded.

"Keith and Maureen soon discovered that the new car was missing," Ella-Mae said. "And their second daughter, Rebecca, had no idea where her sister might be. At first, they thought maybe their daughter had decided to take out the car by herself, but they soon dismissed this theory. Connie had wanted to take the first ride in it with Keith and Maureen, and had made a big deal out of it the night before. Keith and Maureen started calling everybody who they knew to find out if anyone had seen Connie that morning."

"This is terrible," Ruby whispered. "Poor Connie. Poor Keith and Maureen."

"But no one had seen her since her party the night before. Not even Colton, her long-term boyfriend and high school sweetheart, who usually spent morning's with her during the summer—they spend a lot of time at the local beach with friends during summer break."

"I bet it was Colton," Ruby said. "But he's young too. This is just—"

"Keith and Maureen contacted the police to report

their daughter missing, but because 24 hours hadn't passed, the police didn't want to make a missing persons report. Shocking. Nobody seemed to know where Connie had gone. It was as if she'd disappeared. Local volunteers formed search teams, and it was thought that maybe Connie had gone out into the wooded area behind her house, for whatever reason, and had gotten lost. But a search of the surrounding area brought up no results." Ella-Mae sighed. "Until the very next morning."

Ruby gasped. I was on the brink of gasping too, even though I'd already seen this. Ella-Mae was a natural story-teller, that was for sure.

"Connie was found on the beach. She had been murdered, stabbed repeatedly, and that was where the trail went cold. Everyone who could possibly have wanted to murder Connie had an alibi, even her then on-and-off again boyfriend, Colton. A lot of family members and friends are still convinced, to this day, that he was the one who did this, but nobody knows why. Connie's car was never found. Police have classed this as a cold case, but if you have any information—"

I shut off the video. "And that's it."

"I almost can't believe that happened," Ruby said. "It's one thing when we investigate these cases, but when you watch it relayed like that... It's so sad."

"And now, her body has been dug up. I want to know

why. We need to find out if any of Connie's family members are alive. Maybe they can give us new leads or ideas."

"You really think Connioe's cold case is related to the grave robbing?"

"I don't see why not," I said. "It's too much of a coincidence if not. And besides, all of the graves that were dug up seem to be from the same time period. That's got to mean something too."

"Maybe."

I tapped my chin, ruminating over everything we'd discovered. "I think this is our main lead. We find out more about this cold case, and then we'll find out who's disturbing the peace in our town."

Ruby nodded. "I have to admit, after seeing this video, I want to find out the truth and bring Connie's killer to justice."

"Me too." I frowned, and then it hit me like a bolt of lightning. "I think I know what our first lead could be."

"Oh?"

"Rebecca," I said, "the victim's younger sister. I'm banking on her still being alive."

Ten

"Are you sure about this, Bee?" Ruby asked, working her hands against the steering wheel. We were parked outside Rebecca Garderner's, and I had brought a box of donuts from the bakery to give her.

"That's the second time you've asked me that this week," I said. "Are you OK? Usually you're pretty excited about these types of investigations."

"I know," Ruby said, looking up at the double story house that was on the far side of the bay. Clearly, Rebecca had inherited her parents' money, or done really well for herself.

"What's going on?" I shifted in my seat. "What's bugging you?"

"I don't know. I guess I thought that when we sold the food truck, we'd stop investigating these things, and I always worry how it will affect us," Ruby said. "Like, in the future. The bakery and just our lives. I'm finally enjoying my life. I have Jamie, and I have you and—"

"You don't enjoy solving cases anymore," I said.

"It's not that. I do. I just don't want to wind up in any trouble that might have consequences for us, and you heard Detective Rourke the other day," she said. "He clearly thinks we're going to interfere."

I nodded, trying to see it from her perspective. "I know you love investigating," I said. "And I also know that you don't want to ruin things. But I don't see a world in which I'll stop sleuthing if the opportunity presents itself. I'll understand if you don't want to do it anymore."

Ruby gave me a look of shock-horror. "As if I'd let you do this on your own."

"Good to know." I flashed her a smile then got out of the car and headed up to Rebecca's house. The yard was massive and well looked after, and I caught sight of a gardener rounding the corner—so Rebecca could afford help.

I didn't think the sister of the victim would have wanted to dig up her body. Or several others. So I wasn't pre-suspicious of the woman, which was a first for me. I hardly ever gave people the benefit of the doubt when it came to murder.

We were all capable of it, whether in self-defense or in

cold blood.

Ruby joined me on the wooden, wraparound front porch, and I knocked on the door, holding the donuts at the ready.

Rebecca had only been a child when her sister had been murdered. It had to have been a life-changing event for her, if what the video had said was true about their bond. She was just fifty-eight-years old. Still in the prime of her life as far as I was concerned.

I knocked on the front door a second time.

It opened.

Rebecca Gardener was beautiful, with blonde hair in a French braid, dressed in a cream yoga pants and a loose t-shirt. She was the picture of serenity, and she sort of reminded me of a croissant. Tan, but clearly stylish and with a hint of smooth charm.

"May I help you?" Rebecca asked.

Her accent was lightly North-Eastern, but with a hint of something else—like she'd traveled and was happy for others to know it.

"I'm Ruby," my friend said, "and this is Bee. We're from Bee's Bakery in town? We wanted to talk to you about your sister."

I thrust the box toward her. "We're sorry for your loss."

Rebecca looked confused but accepted the donuts,

peering inside. Her face lit up. "Oh, there's custard in them."

"That's right," I said smiling. "Custard-filled, dipped in confectioner's sugar. It's a light vanilla custard, made with vanilla beans fresh from the pod."

"Amazing," Rebecca said. "Thank you. Though, you've caught me by surprise. I was just doing my stretching, and I didn't expect any condolences so long after my sister's passing."

"We thought you had heard about..." Ruby couldn't get the words out.

"The grave robbing incident." Rebecca sighed and shut her eyes. "I've heard, yes. But why are you interested in that?"

Ruby opened her mouth to come up with a pat excuse.

"We're sleuths," I said. "We've solved quite a few murders in our time, and we were curious about your sister's cold case."

"Really?" Rebecca didn't seem upset about our prying yet. "That's something. You've solved murder cases?"

"We were in the newspaper," Ruby said. "The Chief of Police gave us a special award."

"That's fantastic. Forgive me, I don't read newspapers any more. I haven't for a long time. I avoid the news most of the time. Either it gives me a headache or it gives me bad news, and I'd prefer neither of those."

She was nice. A little too nice. *But she would have no motive to dig up graves.*

"Come on in." Rebecca stepped back and gestured for us to enter her foyer.

"You have a lovely home," Ruby said, peering around at the family pictures, the gorgeous rich wood stairs that led up to a second level. The interior was as calm as Rebecca seemed. A croissant house.

"Through here." Rebecca padded, barefoot, I now noticed, into another room.

The living room was open plan, leading into a kitchen that was homey and must have been a dream to cook in. I could picture baking a cake in it, and the leather sofa was comfy. We sat down on Rebecca's urging, and she walked through to the kitchen to make us coffee. The rest of the area was filled with interesting curios and artifacts that must have been her father's.

"What do you want to know?" she asked. "I haven't talked about my sister in years to anyone outside of the family. My mother and father passed a year apart from each other about five years ago. You know, my mother never gave up hope about finding out what happened to my sister."

"That's beautiful," Ruby said.

"Hopefully, we can respect her final wish," I said. "I know you were young at the time it happened, but I wondered if you could tell us if any of the police's suspects are still alive today."

"Oh, sure," she said. "There's me, though I don't count as a suspect since I was a girl at the time, and then there's Matt. He's a mechanic in Mystery. He was friends with my sister when it happened, but he didn't do it either. Had an alibi."

"Was there anyone else?" I asked.

Rebecca paused with the coffee pot in hand, thinking about it. "Only Colton, my sister's boyfriend at the time. But he died of a heart attack years ago. And he had an alibi at the time too, allegedly."

"You sound dubious about that," I said.

"Because I didn't believe his alibi then, and I don't believe it now. Colton murdered my sister. I'm sure of that. I wish we could prove it. You'd think with how far police work and all that DNA stuff has come that they'd have been able to solve the case."

"What was Colton's alibi?" I asked.

"So, his alibi was that he was at the library studying at the time of my sister's death—they can figure that out you know, with tests and so on—but the librarian didn't seem sure she'd seen him there. Like she sort of changed her story after talking to the police. And wouldn't you know it, Colton's father was the detective at the time. So I'm convinced that they squashed it."

"Have you ever talked to the police about the case? Recently, I mean." Ruby leaned forward and accepted the cup of coffee from Rebecca.

"Not recently. I hate to admit it, but I gave up after a while. We tried for years to get them to pay attention, but nobody picked it up, and in the last ten years or so, I haven't bothered. When my mother fell ill, that took precedence over everything else."

I nodded. "What about this Matt guy?"

"Oh, he and I are friends," she said. "He's ten years my senior, but we bonded in more recent years over what happened to Connie. Things like that, the traumatic events in life, they tend to stick you together like glue, because nobody else seems to understand what it was like to go through them."

"So, you'd say Matt's not the grave robbing type then," I said.

Rebecca laughed. "You have a way with words. And no, he's not. And he couldn't have been grave robbing that night because, well, we were together. On a date. At a local restaurant, Grassfed."

So that ruled out Matt as a suspect for the grave robbing. Darn. But he might know something we didn't, and he was a new lead at least. *This one better not be a dead end.*

Eleven

MATT HAD GRACIOUSLY AGREED TO MEET WITH us on Rebecca's urging, and so, that afternoon, he dropped by the bakery and took a table near the counter stocked with cakes and treats. I'd been popping in and out of the kitchen all morning, awaiting his arrival.

He was nothing like I'd expected him to be.

At 71 years of age, he was tall with broad shoulders, an easy smile, and lines around his eyes that belied his age even though he had a youthful demeanor. He was a mechanic, according to Rebecca, but he didn't arrive in overalls nor did he look particularly greasy.

"Matt," I said, approaching the table.

"You must be Ruby," he said.

"Bee." I pointed to my chest, then gestured to my

friend who had just finished serving a customer behind the counter. "That's Ruby."

"Rebecca mentioned you were interested in talking to me." Matt swallowed. "About Connie."

"If it's not too much trouble," Ruby said, having heard the last of his sentence as she'd approached the table. "We're interested in Connie's cold case."

"It's a darn shame the cops never saw fit to do anything about it," Matt said. "Connie and I, well, shoot—" He cut off and swallowed a second time.

"Can I get you a cup of coffee, Mr.—?"

"Mr. Folson," he said. "But you can call me Matt. It's what everyone calls me around here."

"Oh, you're the owner of Folson's?" The mechanic shop that everyone in town went to when their cars broke down.

"That's right," he said with pride. "That's my place. Worked my whole life to get her up and running. And I'd love a cup of coffee, thank you."

"How do you take it?" Ruby asked.

"Regular."

"Be right back." Ruby went off to prepare the drinks, and I trusted that she'd bring back some cake for us. It had been a long day, and I was two yawns away from falling asleep.

I lowered myself into the seat opposite Matt, trying

not to be obvious about my study of him. I could tell he'd been a strong and handsome young man when Connie had gone missing. Strong enough to have murdered her.

"What did you want to know about Connie?" Matt asked. "I'm willing to help. Shoot, I've been waiting for anyone to pay attention to this case. Darn cops don't care. They haven't cared for years."

"Thank you," I said. "We appreciate your help."

"Ayuh. Not a problem."

My angle of approach was simple. Alibi first. "Where were you on the night that Connie went missing?"

"I was at home," Matt said. "My brother and I shared a room, you see, and I was in bed all night. Besides that, Connie was murdered well into the following day."

"She was?"

"According to the police reports at the time, they said her time of death was around 10:00 a.m., that morning. At that time, I was part of the group of volunteers looking for her," Matt paused, shaking his head, a few tears gathering in the corners of his eyes. "It's hard to talk about, even today. Things like that stick with you for life. She was a friend to me during hard times."

"Did Connie say anything to you prior to her disappearance that might've clued you in on what happened later?"

Matt sat back in his seat, folding his arms and considering.

Ruby returned with a tray of coffees and slices of Devil's Food Cake, and we thanked her. My coffee was decaf and my slice was the biggest to help keep me awake during this interview. I shot Ruby a smile of thanks. She was such a considerate person. I had no idea what I'd do without her in my life.

The warm chatter in the bakery and the cozy atmosphere from the decor, yellow golds, and deep brown wood, provided the perfect backdrop for this interview. The bakery would set Matt at ease.

Matt took a sip of his coffee then set it down, brow wrinkled. "I'm trying to recall. The cops never asked me questions like that back then. Only where I was and what I was doin'. But Connie, oh yeah—!"

"What?"

"Connie was acting different in the weeks before it happened, I can say that for sure."

"Different how?" I asked.

"She was upset a lot. Crying. The only time I saw her happy was on her birthday, and that was because she got the ring."

"The ring?" I asked. "What about the car? Wasn't that more exciting for her?"

"Nah." Matt shook his head. "She was obsessed with

that ring her dad gave her. She called me the night before she went missing, right after she got it, and told me how important it was to her. Her parents had her buried with it."

"So she still had the ring when she was found?" I asked, pulling on the thread. Could the ring be the reason a grave robber had dug up Connie's final resting place? It made sense. But that would have to be an exceptionally expensive "secret" ring. Or an exceptionally desperate grave robber.

Matt shook his head. "Connie didn't have the ring on her when she was found. Her parents found it in Rebecca's room when they started searching for her. According to Rebecca, Connie gave it to her for safe-keeping."

"Connie gave her new ring to her kid sister for safe-keeping?" Ruby asked, and I admired the skepticism in her tone.

"Ayuh. My reaction was the same as yours," Matt said. "But the ring was at home. And that struck alarm bells for me 'cos I remember Connie saying she would never take it off. If she did, and she gave it to Rebecca, then it had to have been for a darn good reason. She must have been scared someone would steal it before she left the house that morning. Or before she was taken."

"But there were no signs of forced entry?" Ruby asked.

I took a bite of cake, savoring the sweetness and then shaking my head. "Nope."

"Who do you think did this, Matt?" Ruby asked.

He moved his fork in his plate, clattering it against the porcelain. "Colton," he said, "her boyfriend at the time. They had been fighting before she went missing, and I— It ain't a secret that I had a crush on her back then. I didn't like the guy, and I was sure that he'd killed her. Still sure of it now. I wish I could go back in time now and ask her out before he did. I wish I had taken the opportunity when it was still there. Maybe she would still be alive if I had."

A strange feeling descended upon me, and I forced it away, along with thoughts of Mike.

Regardless, all we'd learned from this conversation was that this ring was important. And that we were out of suspects. Apart from Nate, the security guard, of course.

Twelve

The following morning...

ONCE I WAS SURE THAT LESLIE HAD EVERYTHING under control in the kitchen, and that Ruby was happy to leave Farrah, our server, in charge of the front of house, we left the bakery behind. It was time to gather more information on our only remaining suspect—the security guard.

"It has to be about the ring, right?" Ruby asked. "If what Matt was saying is true, then the ring is the only valuable item that matters."

"Hmm."

"What is it, Bee?"

"I agree with you to a certain degree. The ring seems

like the most likely reason a person would want to dig up Connie's grave, but at the same time, it would have to be a very valuable ring. And why did they dig up three graves?"

"Maybe they got confused in the dark," Ruby suggested, as she unlocked her car and got in. "It could be that they thought they had the right grave, but they managed to dig up the wrong person."

"Two times?" I put on my seatbelt.

Ruby chewed on her bottom lip and started the engine. "Maybe you're right. But... Both those graves were damaged weren't they? Wait, no, one was damaged, the other one was unmarked, and the third was Connie's grave."

"If we could get into the cemetery and check the state of the gravestones, we might be able to tell," I said. "But for now, I say we check out the most obvious lead."

"Nate." Ruby drove us down the road, toward the juice bar, SumFruit, where Nate hung out—according to Leslie.

"As the only person with the keys to the graveyard, it can only be him who either let them in or lost the keys due to negligence."

Ruby made a noise in her throat. "I could see that happening. The guy was half-asleep when we turned up to talk to him."

"Exactly," I said.

"Oh, imagine…"

"Imagine what?"

"I can see it now," Ruby said, as she directed the car into a parking space outside SumFruit. "Nate's fast asleep at this station in the cemetery, and the grave robber sneaks up and steals the keys from his belt. They make a copy and then return them with Nate being none the wiser."

"That's not a bad theory. Difficult to prove, but not a bad theory."

SumFruit was ridiculously cheerful for a place that was meant to serve smoothies and healthy snacks. Call me a skeptic or a sugar addict—right on both accounts—but it was a difficult sell to make rabbit food seem cheerful.

The splashes of bright color on the walls and the happy-faced fruit images were mocking.

Ruby and I took a seat at one of the cushy booths.

"Oh, there's Reese," Ruby said. "Perfect!" She waved her over.

"Ruby!" Reese wore an annoyingly vibrant peak cap to go with her equally objectionable outfit. I didn't envy the servers here. At least we didn't make Farrah wear brightly colored getups. The honeycomb and bee theme was much milder and easier on the eye.

"How are you?" Ruby asked. "How's business been?"

"Oh good, good. It's nice to see you again," Reese said,

but frowned. "Didn't expect it to be in here, though. You don't like smoothies."

"Mulched up, chunky fruit," I said. "What's not to like?"

"You remember Bee?" Ruby nodded toward me.

"Couldn't forget her if I tried."

"That's the spirit," I said. "You heard about the grave robbing, I assume?"

"Ayuh. Everybody in town's heard about it." Reese leaned in. "Heard there's a new detective in town too. He's real angry. Came by here yesterday to talk to a couple of the other girls who work here. They were jumpy after his visit."

"Were you here when he came by?" Ruby asked.

"Not me, no," she said, tucking blonde hair beneath her peak cap, and then clicking her pen over her notepad.

The juice bar wasn't particularly busy, so we had her attention for the time being.

"According to Chrissie, he was asking about Nate, you know, the caretaker at the cemetery?"

"He was?" Ruby's eyes widened, and her gaze flickered toward me.

"What a coincidence," I said. "That's exactly what we wanted to talk to you about."

"Oh, you're investigating what happened?" Reese gestured for Ruby to scooch over with youthful exuberance. She smushed herself into the booth beside my friend and propped her chin in her palm. "I thought you might."

"Apparently, we have a reputation," I said.

"Ayuh. The two bakers from away who like to solve crimes," Reese said, with a giggle. "You're in the paper more than the weather nowadays."

"Not good for keeping a low profile," I replied. "So, you mentioned Rourke wanted to talk to people about Nate?"

"Ayuh." Reese glanced around. "But he didn't talk to me because I wasn't working yesterday. I'm part-time at the moment. Got weddings to plan with Moira out of town."

"She's still not back yet?" Ruby asked.

Reese shook her head. "I know plenty about Nate if you've got questions."

"Define plenty," I said.

"I know that he threw a party at his house the other night. A big one out on Pollard Street, and that the neighbors complained because of the noise," she said. "I know that he's a rig if I've met one, and that he has a long-term girlfriend who was five years younger than him."

"What's her name?" I asked.

"Dewy Phillips," Reese said, with an eye roll. "And she's a rig too." She lowered her voice. "A dubbah too. She acts like the sun shines out of her rear-end because she was popular in high school. Funny thing is, it's not like she grew up rich or anything like that."

"What does that matter?" I asked.

"See, I don't care if people are rich or not, but she's the kind of person who does, and she acts like she grew up rich and like the whole town owes her. She comes in here once a week with Nate, and she acts like she's a queen." Reese arched an eyebrow. "And the last time they were in here together? They started yelling at each other at the top of their lungs. I had to ask them to leave."

"So, their relationship wasn't going well," Ruby said.

"Ayuh. I don't like to interfere in people's business, but those two... They didn't make it difficult to interfere when they were yelling they hated each other in public."

This wasn't exactly a "lead" per se, but it was better than what we'd had when we'd arrived here. Nate had a girlfriend, and he was irresponsible. That didn't necessarily connect with the grave robbing or the cold case, but it was worth asking questions.

An angry girlfriend would surely be happy to give us information about Nate's nightly activities—including those that included flashlights and shovels.

Thirteen

NATE'S HOUSE ON POLLARD STREET WAS ON THE "wrong side of the tracks" as Ella-Mae might've said in one of her WatchMe true crime videos. I couldn't help thinking about her show on the video hosting site with admiration.

It was something I could see myself doing—assuming anyone would want to hear what I had to say.

The house was a tiny square thing with a chain link fence and a gnome lawn ornament that was missing its head and sat, a hollowed out ceramic shell, among the weeds.

A beat up car was parked out front, its blue paint peeling, and the trunk was open and overflowing with black trash bags.

"Well," I said, "this should be fun."

"It's a mess," Ruby whispered. "And what's with the trash bags and the car and—"

The front door of the house opened, and a young woman wearing a tank top and a pair of jean shorts—or 'jorts' as the kids liked to call them—trudged down the steps and onto the cracked concrete path. She dragged her worn flip flops rather than lifting her feet in what had to be the most annoying habit known to man—bar eating with one's mouth open.

She was a greasy donut with day-old glaze and a few sprinkles that did little to add flavor.

"That must be her," Ruby whispered. "The girlfriend."

"Dewy Phillips," I said. "Looks like it, from Reese's description." I hadn't seen her around town. We ran in different circles, and she didn't like baked goods, judging from her figure.

I got out of the Chevrolet as Dewy reached the mound of trash bags spilling out of the car parked out front.

"Dewy Phillips?"

She spun toward me, putting up her fists. "Who's asking?"

"We're private investigators," I said, the untruth slipping off my tongue. "We're looking for Nate. The caretaker at the cemetery."

Dewy lowered her dukes and pulled a face. "None of

my business where he is or what he's doing. Nate and I broke up."

"I'm sorry to hear that," Ruby said. "Are you OK?"

"Fine," she said. "I've been fine. I've been fine since last Thursday. Now, I just want to get my fine butt out of here before he gets home."

"You're leaving?" Ruby asked.

"You blind or something?" Dewy gestured to the car, which we'd both assumed didn't run, and then the trash bags. "Can't you see I'm leaving?"

"And you're taking your trash with you," I said.

"Trash!" She opened one of the bags and reached inside, drawing out another pair of jorts. She shook them at me. "This look like culch to you?"

"I don't think I should answer that question," I said to Ruby as an aside.

"I agree," Ruby replied, before turning to Dewy again. It was better if she handled this. The young woman had gotten on my nerves. "Dewy, we don't mean to bother you, we just wanted to talk about Nate and where he was on the—"

The front door of the boxy house opened a second time, and another young person dragged their feet into view. This one was a dark-haired, hunched over creature who cast surly looks from underneath his brow. He looked

DEVIL'S FOOD CAKE AND DEATH

a few years younger than Dewy, but he had the same sharp nose.

Greasy donut numero dos.

"Warner," Dewy yelled. "Get over here, you dubbah. We're leaving."

He slimed his way down the path and stopped beside Dewy..

"Warner?" Ruby smiled at him. "Nice to meet you. This is your new boyfriend, Dewy?"

"Heck no," she said, and slapped Warner on the back. "This here is my brother, and he's a waste of breath most of the time."

"Shut up, Dewy," Warner breathed.

"You shut up," she said, and slapped him on the back of the head this time. "He came out to help me move my stuff out of Nate's house. Not that you were much darn help, were you? Just stood around doing nothing while I shoved clothes into these bags and—"

"Are we leaving or—?"

"We'll leave when I'm ready," Dewy hissed. "Don't mind him. He's got a bad attitude whenever he has to lift a finger to do anything." She pressed her hair back from her forehead. "Now, what was it you were asking me?"

"About Nate," Ruby said. "And where he was on the night the graves were robbed."

"Right. Hard tellin', not knowin'. I don't spend all my

time here. And I haven't ever since we broke off our engagement. Not that we really had a darn engagement in the first place. He couldn't afford a ring. Had more than enough money to throw himself a big old party every other week, but a ring? That was—"

A window slapped open in the next-door neighbor's house, and an older woman stuck her head out of the window, a cigarette dangling from the corner of her lips. "Hey! You starting up again? I swear, I'll call the cops on you if you make any more noise. I don't have to put up with this, hear me?"

"Relax, you old bat," Dewy shouted back. "We're leaving."

Ruby and I watched the exchange, both with our eyebrows raised.

"See what I have to live with here?" Dewy hefted a final trash bag—zero help offered from her brother—into the trunk of her car then slapped the trunk closed. "We've got to get going. I need to unpack all my things back at home."

"Help me," Warner said loudly, making eye contact with us.

Dewy slapped him on the back of the head and called him a dubbah again before herding him into the car. The pair drove off, trailing exhaust fumes and maleficence.

"That was... something," Ruby whispered.

"Tell me about it," I said. "I'm sure that—"

"Bee?" Mike's unmistakeable baritone came from a few feet behind us.

My treacherous heart crawled up into my throat. He looked as good as always, his beard neatly groomed, two pink spots in his cheeks, and his eyes bright and blue, meeting mine with excitement. "What are you doing out here?"

Ruby muttered something about finding music for the ride back to the bakery and got into the Chevrolet, leaving me and Mike under the blue summery sky.

"We were talking to Dewy Phillips," I said. "Just asking her a few questions about Nate."

"Ayuh. I thought as much. You'd better be careful."

"Careful?"

Mike drew closer. He tucked a lock of my silver-gray hair behind my ear. "Rourke's on a warpath. Wants to whip the town into shape. That's an exact quote." He grimaced. "He doesn't like that you two have been helping out the police department."

"Is that what we're calling it?" I asked.

"I told the captain we ought to hire you two as consultants," Mike said. "Makes the most sense to me."

He was saying all the right things. And it made it that much harder to keep from telling him what we'd discovered. *So tell him then.* And lose my independence. Lose my leads. Mike would have to talk to Rourke about the case. They were partners.

"I've been meaning to catch up with you," Mike said. "Want to go out for dinner this Friday?"

I hesitated. "That sounds great, but I'm not sure if I'm busy or not yet. Can I get back to you?"

"Of course." He leaned in and pressed a kiss to my cheek. "You take care, Bee." And then he strolled up toward the house and knocked on the front door.

I got back into the car, not bothering to tell him that Nate wasn't home.

Fourteen

A THUNDEROUS KNOCKING WOKE ME FROM MY dead sleep.

My eyes flicked open in the half-gloom in my tiny bedroom, and I frowned, pushing myself upright. Caramel yipped a bark from the end of my bed. The knocking came a second time, a banging that penetrated the peace of my little cottage.

"Oh, somebody's head is about to roll," I grunted.

According to Ruby, I was "not a morning person." According to me, I liked what little beauty sleep I could get, and anyone who interfered with that would get the dragon rather than the princess.

I clambered out of bed and into my slippers and robe, casting a bleary-eyed glance at the red numbers on the alarm clock on my bedside table.

It was 07:00 a.m. A devilish hour.

The banging came a third time and was followed by. "Mystery Police Department. Open the door."

That only served to heighten my anger.

I marched out of the bedroom, Caramel following behind me, tail alert.

I wrenched open my front door and found Detective Rourke, his fist raised in his bid to "disturb the peace."

"What on earth are you doing?" I asked. "Have you lost what little mind you have left?"

"Miss Pine," he said.

"That much is obvious. What is not obvious is why you're standing on my front step, ramming your meaty, neanderthal knuckles against the precious wood of my door."

Rourke blinked, temporarily thrown off his game.

"Sorry for waking you, Miss Pine," he said.

"Waking me? Waking me?" The unadulterated audacity of the man. "You didn't wake me. You abruptly ejected me from the REM cycle of my sleep. Did you know it's dangerous to do that to a person? I could have died. I could have had a heart attack. And what then? I suppose you wouldn't have been held liable, would you? So why would you care?"

Caramel let out several yipping barks in support of my argument.

"Something has happened."

"That's true of every second of every day," I said.

Rourke's mean face folded into an expression of intense confusion. If anything, it improved his overall look. "What do—?"

"Right now, something is happening," I said. "That something being you interrupting my sleep and ruining the start of my day. All across the world, things are happening. A bird just pooped on someone's car. A baby is crying. I'd wager somewhere in Australia, someone's fighting a kangaroo. So unless your 'something' is sufficiently important, you had better turn around and leave me to what's left of my shattered morning."

"You *really* don't like being woken up," Rourke said, on the timid back foot.

"Your deductive reasoning skills are astounding. That must be why you're a detective."

Rourke blushed. "Ma'am, a man, Nate Blythe, has disappeared," he said.

Caramel fell silent, and so did I.

It was an important "something" after all.

"And I need to take you down to the station for an interview, as you and your friend were two of the last people to talk to him. And you were seen at his house yesterday afternoon."

I tucked my robe tighter against my chest and let out a

sigh. "You could have led with that," I said. "Give me five minutes to put on some clothes and feed my dog."

AN HOUR LATER, I REGRETTED NOT HAVING spewed more venomous insults in the detective's direction. He'd made me wait while he did whatever it was that useless detective's did to waste one's time.

They had sat me down in their tiny interrogation room—small circular table, bleak walls—given me a cup of awful coffee and a bottle of water and left me to stew.

The funny thing was, I wasn't under arrest. I could leave at any time.

The not so funny thing was, I wouldn't leave because I was desperate to find out more about what had happened to the cemetery caretaker.

The fact that Nate was missing was intensely interesting to me. Either he was missing because someone had done something to him, or he was missing because he had gone on the run. *I like the latter idea.*

It proved that we'd been right about him being the only one who could have done this.

Still doesn't explain why there were multiple flashlights in the cemetery that night I drove past and found Caramel.

Nate hadn't been working alone.

Didn't make sense. Why would he dig up three—?

The door to the interrogation room opened, and Rourke graced me with his presence. He sat down, giving me a scowl. "Miss Pine," he said. "Thank you for offering me your time."

"Nate has gone missing," I said.

"Ayuh. That's correct. I'd like to talk to you about when you last saw him."

I told him about our encounter with Nate at the cemetery and how he'd been asleep. I kept our suspicions about him being the guilty party to ourselves.

"And you were at his house yesterday afternoon. Why?"

"I wanted to ask him a few questions about the grave robbing incident," I said.

"I told you not to do that," Rourke said. "Didn't I?"

"I don't remember anything like that," I replied. "I'm not in the habit of committing irrelevant conversations to memory."

"You realize you're talking to an officer of the law."

"As opposed to an officer of what? The postal service?"

"Miss Pine— "

"There's nothing I can tell you that will help you," I said. "Other than the fact that I believe Nate is on the run. He's likely afraid that you'll arrest him for the grave robbing because he was the only one with the keys to the cemetery."

"And you think you know that for a fact," Rourke said, coming over smug.

"He made a run for it." My convictions stood firm. "And he wasn't at his house when we were there yesterday. Dewy Phillips, however, was. And her brother Warner. I suggest you talk to them."

Rourke didn't write down any notes nor did he look impressed by what I had to say.

"And you know what else?" I was full of that certainty that we were right about Nate.

"I'm sure you're gonna tell me."

"You should look into Connie Gardener's cold case again," I said. "Poor Rebecca has been waiting for years for anyone to solve it, and nothing's come of it. It's pathetic that the local police haven't made an effort, and since you're such a hotshot from the big city, I'm sure your fresh set of eyes would make the world of difference."

"That sarcasm, Miss Pine?" Rourke asked.

"You're the detective." Ruby would've said I was being too angry, too aggressive, but I couldn't abide rude people. Sure, I had my moments, and I was blunt and definitely not without my flaws, but Rourke had been on our case since the get go.

Rourke sat back, his arms folded. "I've already spoken to your friend, Ruby."

"Good," I said. "And she told you the same thing I did, didn't she?"

The detective's mouth turned downward at the corners.

"That's what I thought," I said, rising from my seat. "I assume I'm free to go, unless you want to arrest me, Detective? In which case, I'll more than happily call a lawyer."

"You're free to go."

"Thank you for wasting my morning," I said, then marched from the interrogation room, my nose in the air.

Fifteen

"I don't blame you," Ruby said, from behind the counter in the bakery, later that day. "He got on my nerves too." For once, my friend was firmly in the "throw a milkshake at the annoying detective" camp. It was refreshing that she thought my attitude was right this time around.

"He woke me up." The trouble was, I did have a soft side and a small part of me worried that I had annoyed Rourke so much, he would take it out on Mike. And he didn't need that in his life. He'd already gotten flack from the higher ups in the police department because of the uptick in crime and murders in Mystery.

"He woke us up too. Jamie was furious about it," Ruby said. "He's been staying up late every night writing his book, and he hardly gets sleep nowadays."

"I'm sorry, Rubes," I said. "You know what we need? Devil's Food Cake and iced coffee."

"That's a great idea."

It was the afternoon, and the bakery was in one of the rare lulls where people were down at the beach or at work. There were a couple of busy tables, but most of them were occupied by teenagers on break, and Farrah had a handle on those tables.

I cut up the cake and Ruby made the iced coffees—decaf for me, as per usual. We sat at our favorite table near the gleaming glass cupcake displays. A bite of cake later, and the energy returned to my soul. There was something to be said for a good cake—revitalizing, comforting, joyful. All of these things and more for me.

Part of the pleasure of baking came in tasting the cake afterward. The majority of my satisfaction came from knowing that I was providing others with this feeling. That was the reason why Detective Rourke would *never* get a slice of one of our cakes.

"He's on the run, Ruby," I said. "Nate is on the run, and I'm sure the police know it. They just don't want to tell us anything."

Ruby pulled a face.

"What is it?" I asked.

"Didn't—? No, I'm probably wrong. Maybe I'm just reading too much into things."

"I value your opinion. Come on. Lay it on me. What's your idea."

"Maybe someone did something to Nate," Ruby said. "He might've known something. You know, since he was the only one with the keys to the cemetery. And you said you saw multiple flashlights that night. He could've been working with someone and they got rid of him because he was going to talk," Ruby said.

"You're not wrong. That is definitely a possibility," I said, thinking hard. "We need to find out more about Nate. We need to know whether he was interested in Connie's grave. If he was, he could have dug it up."

"But why?" Ruby asked. "For the ring?"

"That was what Matt seemed to think," I said.

And Matt and Rebecca had alibis for Connie's murder and for the night that the graves had been tampered with —there was no reason for them to lie.

"I guess," Ruby said. "What would Nate's motive be for running, though? Grave robbing is bad, but it's not as bad as murder. And he wasn't even born when Connie was killed. I get the feeling that we're missing something."

I glanced over at the table of teens, who were kidding around, eating cake, and generally ignoring us "old folk." "Then we need to find out what that is," I said. "Sooner rather than later."

"How?"

I took a sip of my decaf iced coffee, followed it up with a bite of my cake, and turned to look at the sunny bay, the people enjoying the sand down below, and the waves that crashed around them.

"I have a plan," I said.

"Uh oh."

THIS WAS THE EPITOME OF RETURNING TO THE scene of the crime for us. We'd gotten into "hot water" with Detective Rourke because we'd decided to come to Pollard Street and talk to Nate. Only to encounter his ex-girlfriend, Dewy.

This time, the house was absolutely silent. The lights were off. The hour was late.

A cool breeze swept through Ruby's car, through our open windows and out again, bringing with it, the scent of the distant ocean, and an atmosphere of promise. That was just my excitement to get in there and find what we needed.

Ruby tugged on a pair of black knit gloves and straightened in the passenger seat. She always got nervous when we did our reconnaissance missions, so I had opted to drive us over to Nate's house.

"I'm sweating like a turkey before Thanksgiving,"

Ruby said. "These gloves are too much."

"At least we don't live in Louisiana. Our heat is a few percent less humid."

"Oh yeah, I can really feel the few percent," Ruby retorted.

"I can tell it's past your bedtime. Let's make this quick, shall we."

Ruby blew her hair out of her face. "Seriously. I don't think I've ever been this sweaty."

My friend usually wasn't overdramatic or irritable like this. Something was definitely bothering her lately, but we'd deal with it later. Jamie's work had annoyed her, was my guess.

I exited the car and strode up the cracked concrete path toward the front of Nate's boxy little house. Ruby followed me, huffing and puffing with every step. I made sure my gloves were in place then tried the front door. Locked.

But Nate was a rather negligent guy, if his sleep schedule at work was to be trusted—and the fact that three graves had been robbed on his watch. My bet was he'd hidden a spare key in plain sight.

"Got it," Ruby hissed, a minute later, lifting a key from inside the hollow ceramic gnome in the front yard.

"That's more imaginative than I gave Nate credit for," I said. "Bravo, Nate."

Ruby brought the key over and we let ourselves into the house. The smell of stale beer and cigarette butts accosted my nostrils. I wriggled my nose and shut one eye as I adjusted to both the odor and the dark.

"At least the house isn't too big," Ruby whispered. "We should be able to search it quickly."

On that note, we split up, bringing out our phones and switching on the flashlight apps. Ruby took the right side of the house and I took the left. We had to make this quick—a neighbor might have seen us creeping up to the house.

The living room was mostly empty apart from an ashtray full of cigarettes, a single sofa, and a small TV. The kitchen had an air of disuse, and the fridge was broken and empty except for a crushed beer can.

The bathroom was—

Not a bathroom at all.

There was a toilet, yeah, but the entire wall above it had been plastered with newspaper clippings and pictures. "Ruby," I whispered out of the bathroom door. "You've got to see this."

My friend appeared, wide-eyed in the relative darkness. I shone my flashlight beam over the wall of clippings. Ruby gasped, her hand going to her throat. "Bee. Is that—?"

"Connie," I said, directing the light at a picture of the

cold case victim, smiling down at us. "Every single one of these images and clippings is about her and her murder. He had to have been collecting them for ages."

And this further proved my theory that Nate had been involved. And that he'd gone on the run to get away from the cops.

Sixteen

The following morning...

IN ORDER TO HELP PROVE MY THEORY, A TRIP TO the cemetery was necessary. Ruby had already driven to the bakery to open it for the day, so I took a leisurely stroll with Caramel on the end of his new lead toward the Mystery Cemetery.

"Nice morning," I said. "Don't you think?"

Caramel yipped an enigmatic response.

"Yeah, perfect day for a walk and an adventure." It was early, just past 06:30 a.m., but the sun was already up, and a few cars drove by, heading toward the bay and the hotspot that would be the restaurants, bakeries and cafes.

Summer in Mystery was like no other that I'd experienced so far. People were in a great mood or a foul one, and there were parties on the beach every Friday night.

The Mystery Cemetery came into view, and the police lines were, thankfully, no longer in place. The gates were open, and the place itself was empty apart from a few visitors who wandered up the paved center path. White, gray, black and marbleised tombstones were spread between trees and surrounded by neatly trimmed green grass.

Say what I wanted about Nate, he'd kept the place neat and tidy.

Caramel whined beside me, and I glanced down at him. "What's wrong, dear?"

The dog plonked his furry butt on the pathway and refused to enter the cemetery a step further. He whined at me, wagging his tail feebly in comparison to his usual enthusiasm.

The cemetery. Of course.

This was where I had first found Caramel. Waiting outside the cemetery for whoever was inside. Did that mean Caramel had belonged to Nate? Or did it mean that he had belonged to whoever else had been robbing the graves?

No, it was definitely Nate. It had to be, after what we'd found in his home, there was no way it could be anyone else. He had been obsessed with Connie's case.

"It's OK, Caramel," I said. "You'll be fine. What if I carry you inside?" I lifted him into my arms and he snuggled against my chest.

I entered the cemetery and Caramel didn't let out a peep of noise. He peered around with his gorgeous brown eyes, taking everything in.

"Let's see," I said. "We're looking for the graves that were—"

"You looking for those graves that were tampered with, you're in the wrong part of the cemetery." The voice drawled from our left, near the caretaker's hutch. An older gentleman stood there, leaning on a rake and wearing a pair of ill-fitting overalls.

"What's your name?" I asked.

The man smoothed a hand over his chest, his bushy white eyebrows prominent, his nose aquiline. "Steve," he said. "Not that it matters a darn bit to you. You're here just like the rest of 'em. Here to see what happened to them graves. Bunch of dubbahs, the lot of you, acting like you're from away. Like you never seen a grave been robbed before."

"It's fair to say that most of us haven't."

"But then, you are from away. I can hear it in your voice." He sucked his teeth. "Fifteen years."

"Fifteen years, what?" I asked, and Caramel shifted in my grip.

"Fifteen years I've been waiting for them to fire that good-for-nothing who worked here. Fifteen years waiting for them to realize what a—" Steve paused and waved a hand. "Nevermind. It don't matter now. Graves you're looking for are further in. Take the path all the way to the big willow. Walk ten paces past it. You'll find the first of them right in front of you."

"And the others?" I asked.

"They're all clustered together," he said, gesturing once, twice, and a third time with his rake. "Just like that. In a straight line. Makes a person think. Makes a person think real hard about the why and the how." He gave me a wry smile that showed he was missing his two front teeth.

"Thanks," I said, and walked off, holding Caramel tighter.

"Nice dog you got there," Steve called after us.

I ignored that comment and stroked Caramel's ears, frowning at everything the man had said. If I'd been a suspicious woman—which I was—I'd add him to my suspect list. What kind of talk had that been? Talking about the graves and the reason they'd been disturbed.

I followed Steve's directions, regardless of his eccentric behavior, and found the first of those graves as directed.

They had been carefully filled in again, but the grass was gone, and the three graves that had been disturbed stood out plainly.

Caramel let out a tiny bark.

"We're fine." I petted his head, frowning at the tombstones.

The first was unmarked as Jo and Haley had indicated it would be. The second was the badly damaged tombstone, lacking a name, and the third...

My eyes widened.

Connie's name was nowhere on it. The only item on the grave was an epitaph that read, "For peace, for patience, always remembered."

It looked as if there had once been a plaque on the tombstone that was no longer there or had been ripped off long ago. Red runnels made the case for the screws that had held the plaque in place having rusted badly.

"It was removed." I sucked in a breath, drawing another small bark from Caramel. "It was removed," I repeated in a whisper. "This is why Nate dug up the wrong graves. He clearly knew that Connie had been buried in one of these spaces, but he wasn't sure which one. So he dug up all three. He must've known she had been buried in an unmarked grave, but didn't know which. This is it! We're on to something."

Caramel's bark had a little more confidence this time.

"We've got to tell Ruby," I said. "And then we're going to call that Detective Rourke and give him a piece of our mind." I turned and hurried past the willow and back onto the long path out of the cemetery.

BY THE TIME I REACHED THE STREET THAT HELD the bakery and overlooked the bay, it was already 07:00 a.m. The minute I turned the corner, I could tell something was amiss.

Caramel padded along beside me, sniffing the air as if he could sense it too.

The bakery doors were closed and Ruby's Chevrolet was parked outside, but that wasn't the problem. A huge crowd had gathered on the pier that overlooked the beach. People were staring at something down there. Staring and talking.

And Ruby was among them!

I rushed across the road, along the embankment and onto the pier to join her, Caramel's paws clattering on the wooden planks.

"What's going on?" I asked.

"You won't believe it," Ruby whispered. "It's just so horrible."

"What?" I followed her stare, and my stomach churned. My hand went to the pocket of my jeans where I kept my phone.

Down on the beach, in plain view of everyone, was a body.

The body of Nate, the caretaker.

"Has anyone called the police?" I asked.

"We called 911. They're on their way," Ruby said. "Bee, you realize what's happened, don't you?"

I surreptitiously took a picture of the body zooming in on it to get as much detail as possible. I couldn't see any stab wounds or blunt force trauma or—

"It's just like Connie."

"Hmm?"

"Connie," Ruby whispered. "She went missing, remember? And then the next day, she turned up on the beach."

Seventeen

A LONG DAY AT THE BAKERY HAD ENDED WITH Detective Rourke dropping by to "check in on us" and make sure we were "fine" after having seen the dead body.

Him caring about how we felt was about as likely as my theory that Nate had been the grave robber.

That was to say, not likely at all.

My assumption had been incorrect, and a part of me wanted to throw in the towel completely. Where had I gone wrong? I had been so sure that I could figure this out on my own, and it had back-fired.

"Bee?" Jamie sat across the table from me, his arm looped around the back of Ruby's chair.

We had eaten a delicious carpaccio paired with a summer fruit salad that didn't at all suit my mood. Not that I blamed him for it. How was he supposed to know I had a metaphorical thundercloud over my head?

"It's been a rough day," Ruby said, smiling at her husband.

"That's a polite way of saying I failed completely."

"Don't be like that." Ruby snapped the words out then colored, and shook her head. "Sorry, I don't know what's gotten into me lately. One second I'm weepy, the next I want to bite someone's head off."

"You're stressed," I said. "There's the bakery to contend with, and then there's this ridiculous grave robbing and now Nate is dead on top of that and—"

"I have an idea," Jamie said. "Why don't you two stay in here and do some brainstorming. I'll do the washing up and pour you both a glass of cold lemonade."

"That would be amazing, honey." Ruby fluttered her eyelashes at her husband.

He kissed her on the forehead, and she went pink again, this time her eyes welling up. She fanned her face and sighed. "Don't know why I'm like this."

Cookie raced into the room and leaped onto the table skidding across it and coming to a halt in front of us. He was in a playful mood, and he batted at the centerpiece—a glass vase filled to the brim with flowers.

"Oh, Cookie, not now," Ruby said.

Cookie raced off again, and Caramel barked from the

corner of the room and chased after the cat, playing right along with him. They were in a good mood.

Ruby placed her phone on the table and opened the app she used to take our case notes. I circled the table and stood behind her, watching as she typed things out, hoping that what she had to say would spark something.

First victim—Connie Gardener. She was murdered in 1967. She went missing and then turned up dead on the beach. Her case has never been solved, and her sister says that she firmly believes it was Connie's boyfriend at the time who killed her.

Matt—He was Connie's friend and had a crush on her. Has an alibi for both the grave-digging and for Connie's time of death. But does he have an alibi for what happened to Nate?

Rebecca Gardener—Connie's sister. She definitely didn't have anything to do with it, but also, we don't know whether that's true of what just happened to Nate.

Second victim—Nate Blyth. He was the local caretaker at the cemetery and was rather lazy. Had an obsession with Connie's death. But why? And who would have wanted to murder him? His body was found on the beach in much the same manner as Connie's. A copycat killer? Or the real murderer?

"And that's all we've got so far. No other suspects," Ruby said.

I studied her notes, frowning and tapping my chin. "Hmm."

"What are your thoughts?" Ruby asked.

"I think that working out who the grave robbers were won't be as easy as working out what happened to Nate. Meaning that we should set the cold case aside for a moment and think about who might have wanted to get Nate out of the way. And why."

"OK." But Ruby didn't instantly open her mouth and come up with ideas. Not that I had any either.

This was frustrating beyond measure.

"The first people we'll need to talk to are those who might've seen him last."

"So probably his ex-girlfriend, Dewy, then?" Ruby made a note of that. "And her brother too. They seemed to know him well. We could also ask Leslie if she knew anyone else who was close to him. Though, I suppose we already covered that. When we asked her the first time, she told us he hung out in SumFruit."

"Yeah." But there had to be more to this. We were missing something, and this felt an awful lot like we had to go right back to square one, before we'd even started looking into what had happened in the cemetery.

"Matt mentioned the ring might be important," I said. "Maybe the grave robber was looking for the ring. Nate might have been one of the grave robbers, and, like you surmised before, the other one decided to get rid of him. They didn't know which grave to rob because none of them had the correct names on them any more."

"So, that gives us a motive, but—"

"It still doesn't tell us who murdered Connie or who murdered Nate," I said.

Ruby nodded.

"Everything going OK here?" Jamie had returned with our promised glasses of lemonade. "I come bearing refreshments."

"Thank you so much, honey."

"You're a star, Hanson." I took the lemonade from him and drank deeply, the coolness refreshing me to the core. This was a frustrating scenario, but I couldn't let it beat us. Or me.

I sent up a silent prayer for help.

"We'll talk to Dewy tomorrow," I said. "She might be able to give us Nate's last whereabouts."

"That's a good idea." Ruby took a sip of her lemonade. "We'll follow the clues, like we always do, and we'll figure it out. Don't worry, Bee. We've got this."

I had my doubts. I just *could not* see how it was all connected, no matter how hard I tried.

Eighteen

FINDING OUT WHERE DEWY PHILLIPS STAYED
wasn't too challenging—a quick call to Leslie had given us
the information. Ironically enough, Dewy and her brother
lived just down the street from Nate, so the big deal she'd
made about moving seemed suspicious in hindsight.

Ruby hummed under her breath as she directed the car
down the street, casting a smile in my direction once in a
while. "We're going to figure this out, Bee."

She'd been repeating the mantra this morning. Obvi-
ously, I wasn't doing a good job of hiding my emotions.

Frustration had to be written all over my face and radi-
ating from my person.

I had been so *darn* sure that Nate was the one who
had dug up those graves. It made sense. The newspaper
clippings in his home, the fact that he was the only one

with the keys to the cemetery, and even the fact that he didn't live in the best part of town and was probably short on cash.

"Here we are," Ruby sang, parking in front of another of those boxy houses on Pollard Street.

The beat up blue car was in the driveway, the trunk shut this time, and it was clear that Dewy and her brother took a little more care of their home than Nate had. Marginally. There was no broken gnome on the front lawn, but the grass was dry and sparse.

I sat for a moment.

"Bee?"

"Hmm?"

"Are you OK? Usually, you're already out of the car by the time I unclip my seatbelt."

"Just thinking about the case and what's ahead," I said.

"What's ahead?"

"Disappointment if I can't figure this out." I folded my arms then unfolded them again, struggling to get comfortable in the moment or in my body for that matter. "I wanted to solve this case on my own. With you, of course."

"Why?"

Why? That's a good question. "Because a part of me wants to prove that I can do it. And to make Robert proud." My throat closed, and I shook my head at myself.

"And because I just can't... I can't trust that Mike or anyone else will be able to do it."

"Bee," Ruby said then hesitated.

"What?"

"Bee, do you think maybe you're so obsessed with the case because you're afraid of Mike."

"Me? Afraid of a *man*?" I scoffed.

"Yeah. You're afraid of how much you like him," Ruby said.

I fell silent.

"Come on, Bee, every time I mention his name you change the subject. You know, I never met Robert, but I believe that he would have wanted you to be happy, right?"

I nodded, unable to formulate a verbal response.

"And if being with Mike will make you happy, then that's what Robert would want. I don't think he'd want you to push that opportunity away or to prove your independence to him. But what do I know? Like I said, I never met the guy." Ruby paused. "It's just, from everything you've told me, he seemed like a good man."

"The best," I croaked.

"The best," Ruby said. "And then I have to be right, don't I? About him wanting you to move on and be happy."

Tears stung my eyes—treacherous emotions. "But how

can I do that when his case was never solved? How can I—?"

"I don't know," Ruby replied, her face open and honest. "But the longer you hang onto the past, the more you struggle to stay in the present and enjoy the time you have with all of us now. It's not going to last forever. Gosh, if these cases have taught me anything it's that."

She had a point.

A door banged nearby, and I wiped away the tears that had spilled onto my cheeks.

"Look," Ruby whispered, pointing at the blue car. "The brother."

Warner glided toward the car, his prominent nose leading, and his phone in his hand. He texted idly and stopped, fiddling in the pocket of his loose jeans then bringing out a set of car keys.

I got out of Ruby's Chevrolet and went over. "Warner," I said.

He jumped and dropped his keys. "What the—? You tryna give me a heart attack?"

"Sorry," Ruby called, as she shut her car door. "We didn't mean to startle you."

"What do you want?" he asked, sour as a lemon rind.

"Is your sister around?" I asked. "We wanted to talk to her about what happened to Nate."

"No, she ain't around." Warner picked up the keys and

juggled them from one hand to the other. "She got herself in trouble because of Nate. Always knew it would happen. I always said that Nate was up to no good."

"No good?" Ruby asked.

"Ayuh. He had this wall of—well, it ain't my place to say, but he was obsessed with dead people. That's why he worked at the cemetery and all." The jingle of keys passing from his one palm to the other punctuated his words. "Anyway, Dewy's at the police station. They're questioning her because he went and got himself killed. Probably because of that grave robbing stuff."

"You think he had something to do with that?" I asked.

"Ayuh. Everybody does. He was obsessed, like I said. Other night at the party, he kept talking about having a friend in the cemetery. What a rig. Rest his soul and all that." Warner inserted the keys into his car door and unlocked it. "Got to go pick up some groceries. Come back later if you want to talk to Dewy. Assuming they don't arrest her."

I strode back to Ruby's car, mulling over what he'd said.

Once we were safely inside the Chevrolet, I turned to my friend. "A friend in the cemetery," I mused. "Could it be? Hmm."

"What?" Ruby's gaze followed Warner's car as it drove off.

"Let's take a drive past the cemetery, Ruby, just so I can think. Hmm..." Could it be as simple as that?

Ruby didn't ask any further questions, sensing that I needed time with my thoughts. She drove us into town and past the cemetery gates, which were open. Inside I caught a glimpse of Steve near the care taker's hutch, a pair of shears in his hands. He didn't notice us watching.

"Who's that?" Ruby asked.

"Steve," I said. "Remember, I told you about him?"

"The new caretaker."

"Yeah. The one who might have a solid motive for having wanted Nate out of the way," I said. "Steve wound up getting a job after Nate died, and he had nothing good to say about him."

"And he could be the friend at the cemetery that Warner just told us about." Ruby's tone was filled with excitement.

"He could be," I said. "He could be." But my gut said something was missing here. If Steve had been Nate's friend at the cemetery, then that had to mean that Steve had already been hanging around the cemetery a lot.

That or Steve wasn't the friend—which made sense since he'd only gotten the job after Nate had died.

We drove back down the street and past the cemetery.

This time Steve stood just inside the gates, staring at us as we passed, his eyes narrowed to slits.

Ruby jolted, and slammed her foot down on the brakes accidentally, then sped up again, her tires squealing. "Sorry," she hissed. "I got the fright of my life when I saw him standing there like that. It's like he knew what we were thinking."

Like he knew what we were thinking. If only I had more information that tied Steve to Nate and the case of grave robbing.

I knew who to call.

Nineteen

That night...

KNOWING WHO TO CALL AND ACTUALLY GOING through with the call were two different issues entirely. Ruby's words from earlier in the day had stuck with me, and the more I thought about them, the more they sounded true. And embarrassing.

I'd spent the entire day baking with Leslie, ruminating about the cold case, the new case, and the grave robbing. It was good to get my thoughts in a semblance of order, but it had also been a great tactic for avoiding what needed to be done.

I checked the time on my phone—just past eight at

night—then placed my hand on Caramel's head where he lay beside me on the sofa in my cottage.

Over the past week, I hadn't received any care packages on my doorstep—before we'd started dating, Mike had left me a series of gifts in front of my cottage door, ranging from chocolates to flowers to notes.I hadn't heard from Mike since he'd last suggested we go out for dinner. He was busy with the case.

"So, giving him a call isn't a bad idea," I said to Caramel.

He whined and wagged his tail. He'd picked up some weight since he'd started staying with me. Caramel liked his sleep and his play and was a sweet dog. A fact that only made me angrier when I thought about how I'd found him.

"What do you say?" I asked him. "Do you think I should give him a call? He might know something about the—"

My phone buzzed as a text message popped through.

Ruby had sent me a link to an article. "Your suspicions about the ring were right!" She had typed that out with a smiley face afterward.

I opened the link she'd sent. It directed to the online version of *the Mystery Mail*—the local newspaper.

Murder and Mayhem in Mystery! Graves desecrated. Rings stolen.

By the Mystery Mail, July 25.

Chaos broke out over the past week in Mystery, when three graves were robbed by what appears to be the caretaker of the cemetery, Nate Blythe. According to sources close to the police, several rings were taken from the bodies of the deceased and may have been the motive for the crime. A request for comment from the Mystery Police Department went unanswered.

Nate Blythe's body was found this week on the beach near the pier in Mystery, with the cause of death as yet unknown. The Mystery Mail will update this page as information is provided to us. Any clues, evidence or information which may lead to an arrest should be reported directly to the Mystery Police Department hotline.

"Ha," I said and petted Caramel. "So Nate was after the ring. The one that Matt told us was important for whatever reason."

And that made talking to Mike easier. I could reveal my evidence to him at last, and do what Ruby had said. Let go of my fears and trust that Robert would approve of this.

I shut my eyes for a second, inhaling deeply through my nose. I set aside my fears then unlocked my phone and dialed Mike's personal number.

He picked up after the second ring. "Bee?"

"Mike," I said. "Sorry I didn't get back to you sooner about a dinner date. How are you?"

"Busy." His tone was gruffer than usual. "Case is complicated. Rourke is... Rourke."

"Ah." I nodded.

An awkward silence followed that.

"I help you with something?" he asked. "I'm working late, and I'd like to get back to it."

"Well, now that we're on the topic," I said, "I wanted to talk to you about what I know."

"What you know about what?"

"The case. Both the cold case of Connie Gardener, and the death of Nate Blythe."

A hesitation and then, "I'm listening."

I broke down the facts, clearly and took my time in explaining exactly what I thought was going on. That Steve might be a suspect. That Dewy and her brother could have had something to do with it. That the rings were important and the motive. That more than one person had been at the cemetery that night.

"How do you figure that?" Mike asked, in his low growl.

"I was there."

"You were... What?"

"I drove past the cemetery on my way home from work the night the graves were being robbed. I know for a fact that there was more than one person in there. There were at least two flashlight beams moving around in the darkness. Now, I'm sure one of them was Nate's, but the other one... That's what I'm trying to figure out. I wondered if you had any information to share with me."

"You want me to share information with you, which I'm not 'sposed to do—"

"You always share information and clues with Ruby and me."

"—after you kept a vital clue from me? I could've used this information about the multiple flashlights sooner."

"I—"

"Why did you keep it from me? You should've told me the minute it happened. Could've prevented all of this."

"Mike—"

"Thank you for the new information, Miss Pine. I'll send an officer over to take your statement in the morning."

"Mike—"

"I have to get back to work."

"Oh, come on!" I snapped, throwing up a hand. Caramel barked. "It's not like you guys have been doing your due diligence either."

"We've been doing our jobs," he grunted.

"Except when it comes to Connie's cold case," I replied. "What about that? Rebecca and Matt have been waiting for answers for years. They've wanted the truth, and you haven't given that to them."

"That's before my time," Mike said. "I—"

"You could open the case. You could investigate it again."

"You're changing the subject. If you'd told me about those flashlights sooner, we might have changed how we went about investigating the case."

"There has to have been other evidence that pointed toward it," I said. "More than one set of footprints or—"

"There was nothing," Mike replied. "Knowing that changes a lot."

A sinking feeling started in my gut. That ball of iron was back, and it pressed downward, pulling me into the sofa, toward the earth. "I didn't think it was a big deal."

"Next time you know something, say something," he said, and then he hung up, leaving me with that cold sinking feeling that I had ruined everything.

Caramel crawled into my lap and sat with his furry paws on my thighs, peering up into my eyes with an enigmatic look. He wagged his tail and licked my chin, while I stared directly ahead, my heart beating wildly.

"This is bad," I whispered. "This is bad. I have to fix this."

Twenty

The following morning...

"ARE YOU SURE YOU DON'T WANT TO COME WITH me?" I asked.

Ruby finished preparing a cup of coffee behind the machine in the bakery and placed it carefully on a tray. She rang a bell for Farrah, and our cheerful server—she reminded me of a chocolate fondant because of her warm and sweet attitude—came over and collected it.

"I'll hold down the fort today, Bee. I think this is something you need to do."

How was it she understood me so well? "If you're sure."

"I'm sure. You go and... I want to say have fun, but I'm not sure you will." Ruby handed me her car keys.

"We'll see. Thanks for this." I waved goodbye with the car keys, and then headed out the doors of the bakery. I'd finished my baking for the morning, and if there were any orders that needed fulfilling, Leslie would handle them.

If I could figure out what had happened to Nate or find another verifiable lead for Mike, it would go some way to helping make up for my previous silence. In retrospect, I should have told him what I knew straight away, but I'd had my reasons. I would apologize for it, but I'd had my reasons.

A short car ride later, I arrived at the gorgeous sprawling home that belonged to Rebecca.

The garden was as immaculate as the last time we'd visited her, but the front door was open, and a wariness descended upon me.

It was a possibility that whoever wanted that ring—this had to be the most priceless ring in the world, for heaven's sake—would come looking for Rebecca next since they hadn't found it in Connie's grave.

I parked the car, hopped out and strode up to the house.

It was silent inside, apart from a gentle thrum of music from another room. I knocked once on the door.

The music stopped abruptly, and footsteps padded out

into the hall. Rebecca, her blonde hair in a French braid, looking particularly croissant-like, emerged, holding a guitar in one hand.

"Oh, Bee," she said. "You're back. Come in."

I stepped inside, eyes narrowing. "Your front door was open. Was that intentional?"

"Yes, it's going to be blindingly hot today according to the radio," she said. "I want to circulate fresh air before I close up the house and turn on the air-conditioning. Close it if you want."

I entered and shut the front door, locking it with a loud clack. "You need to be more careful, Rebecca."

"Careful? Why? I'm not afraid of a grave robber."

"Didn't you hear about Nate?"

"Nate?"

"The care taker at the cemetery has been murdered," I said. "In the same way as your sister was killed."

Rebecca gasped and nearly dropped her guitar. She caught it before the neck slipped from her grasp and placed it against the wall. "I—I had no idea. He's dead?"

"He went missing and then turned up on the beach, just like Connie."

"That's terrible." Rebecca gestured for me to follow her through to her lovely open plan kitchen and living room. "Please, sit. Can I get you something to drink?"

"I'm good, thanks."

"So what happened? The caretaker is dead?"

"Yes," I said. "And it's definitely connected to what happened to your sister. It can't be a coincidence. Connie died in such a specific way."

"I agree. But why?"

"I have a theory that Nate was one of the grave robbers who tried to get into your sister's grave," I said. "I believe that he was looking for her ring. Her "secret" ring. And that his accomplice, whoever they may be, decided to get rid of him because he knew too much about their plan."

"That's something, all right," Rebecca said.

"I can't figure out why the ring would be so important," I said. "Do you know anything more about the ring or its whereabouts?"

Rebecca hesitated, and a thrill ran down my spine. She knew something that she wasn't telling me. For a second, I regretted closing and locking the front door. Rebecca could be the murderer in disguise.

But no. She certainly hadn't killed her sister. And she had an alibi for the night of the grave robbing. She had been out with Matt at Grassfed. A quick call had verified that—I did my police work and my baking thoroughly.

"What is it, Rebecca?" I asked. "You're not telling me the whole story, are you?"

"As you know," Rebecca said, glancing around at the room and the many curios in it, "my father was an archaeologist. An adventurer. He collected curios where he could, but being an archaeologist didn't always pay well."

"I can imagine."

"My mother was well off. She was a doctor, but my father, well, he was always looking for a way to make more money. But he wanted it to be easy rather than hard," Rebecca said. "He got into business with a few shady characters over time, trading, well, frankly... old artifacts, gold, even diamonds."

My eyebrows arched. This was not what I'd expected to hear when I'd arrived at the house.

"He wanted us, my sister and I, to inherit what he'd found or... stolen, without anyone knowing. He gifted Connie a ring. A special ring that contained a clue within it to the whereabouts of his 'treasure' as he liked to call it." Rebecca lifted her hand and grasped a golden chain around her neck. She lifted it showing off two rings at the end. "And on my twenty-first birthday, he did the same for me. Two rings with different clues in them that would lead to the truth."

"But Connie's ring was buried with her."

"It wasn't," Rebecca said. "My father made sure it wasn't. All this time, I've had it in my possession, Both rings, and both clues. Not that they matter any more. I've already found the riches and moved them."

"So the grave robbers were looking for a ring that

I said. "But how could they possibly
know that?"

Rebecca shook her head. "Everyone in town knew that
Connie's ring was valuable. There was even a rumor going
around at the time that she had been buried with money.
It was ridiculous, of course, but there you have it. That's
the truth. I haven't told anyone about it except for you.
Not even Matt."

"Why?"

"Because of the nature of my father's business. And
what do you think would happen if I came out and said
that? I'd lose everything," Rebecca said. "I'm basically an
accessory to a crime. And goodness, hasn't my life been
hard enough? I lost my sister. Both my parents are dead.
Can you really say you wouldn't do the same, given the
opportunity?"

I thought about it and found that I couldn't. "Did the
old cemetery caretaker know about the ring?"

"Tenny? Why, yeah, I imagine he did. He was there
when my sister was buried, and he worked in the cemetery
for years."

"Hmm."

This was more than enough. New information that I
could give to Mike as a peace offering. I'd just have to be
careful about it and not sell out Rebecca in the process.
"Thank you," I said to her. "Thank you for your honesty.

I'm working on getting the police to pay more attention to what happened to your sister."

"The more the days pass, the more strongly I feel about finding her killer," Rebecca said, her eyes teary. She pressed her hand over the rings. "If I trust anyone, it's you."

Twenty-One

THE MYSTERY POLICE DEPARTMENT WAS SMALL and gray inside—not a place I would've wanted to work. The receptionist directed me toward Mike's office, which was near the back of a bullpen that contained a few officers working their desk jobs. A couple of them were familiar faces and greeted me with a nod or a smile.

I smiled back, even though that iron ball had dropped into my stomach again.

Mike could very well reject me, and I couldn't say I didn't deserve that. But this was about the case. And he would surely appreciate the extra information that Rebecca had given me.

Mike's office door bore a plastic plaque that read "Detective Mike Winters", and had a window beside the door with blinds drawn. A palpable sense of frustration drifted from the shut door.

I knocked on it once.

"Come in," Mike called out, gruffly.

I entered and found him seated behind his desk, a mound of paperwork stacked neatly in his in-tray, and his gaze fixed on a computer screen. He clicked repeatedly with a yellow-cream mouse and adjusted a pair of reading glasses on the tip of his nose before looking up at me. "Bee," he said. "What are you doing here?"

"You would have preferred Detective Rourke instead?" I smiled again, but the iron weight was still there.

"Not sure how to answer that. But Rourke never knocks when he comes by my office, so I knew it wasn't him. Shut the door. Take a seat."

I did as he'd said, placing my handbag in my lap and fiddling with its clasps. "I'm sorry, Mike," I said. "I should have told you about the lead sooner, and I should have responded to your invitation to dinner as well."

He grunted but didn't say anything.

"I'm still getting over what happened to my husband," I said, lifting my chin. "I don't know how long that's going to take me, but I am working on it. I see the error of my ways now."

Again, he didn't say anything.

"I hope you'll accept my apology, but if not, I understand that too." And then I let out a breath.

"Thank you," he said. "I appreciate it. Sorry if I made you feel pressured about dating."

"No, no, you haven't. It's a personal problem."

The silence started up between us, and I continued fiddling with the clasps obsessively. "I have information for you," I said. "Something I found out today."

"You do?" Mike sighed. "I could use anything you have. I need a break in this case. Rourke's been on my behind like a prosthetic lobster tail."

I snorted a laugh. "That can't be pleasant."

"Ayuh, 'bout as pleasant as it sounds. What did you find out?"

I told him about Rebecca and her ring. That she had kept it, and that it was suspected that the motive for Nate having robbed her grave was that he wanted that ring. I didn't tell him about the illegal treasure stash, but it wasn't important and might get Rebecca in trouble.

"I appreciate that," Mike said. "It helps knowing where the ring is. Might be that the killer tries to track it down."

"Do you have any leads on that?" I asked.

Mike was open with me, but I wasn't sure he would be after the way I had acted.

He scratched the back of his head then removed his

glasses and inserted one of the temple tips between his teeth, considering. "This is a mutually beneficial relationship," he said. "Or it was. You tell me what you've got, and I tell you what I've got. We work together. Rourke would have a litter of kittens if he found out I was talking to you. But Rourke can kiss the back-end of a raccoon for all I care." Mike huffed out a breath. "I need a break. In the case. Maybe from work, but right now, in the case."

"I can help you brainstorm."

"Here's what I've got," he said, this time without hesitation. "I've got the dead body of a man who robbed the graves he was meant to care for. We have evidence proving that, and now, thanks to your testimony, evidence that he wasn't working alone."

Great. I'd been right about Nate being the grave robber.

"I've got Nate's house trashed," Mike continued. "Turned upside down just this morning as the murderer looks for the ring, is now my assumption. We knew the rings were taken, but not that they were never there."

"Wait, rings?"

"Ayuh. One ring removed from each of the bodies. Except the last one, Connie's, apparently."

"Please continue." I had stopped fiddling with the clasps on my handbag, intensely focused on what he had to say.

"I have three main suspects, two with alibis, one without. Can you guess who they are?" Mike asked.

I liked a challenge. "Dewy Phillips," I said, "the ex-girlfriend because she might have a motive to have murdered him. The brother, Warner, because he knew about Nate's obsession or might have helped his sister. And... Steve? The new caretaker?"

"Right on all accounts. But Dewy and Warner have alibis. They were with each other at the time that Nate went missing, and they were spotted in SumFruit. We're waiting on the exact time of murder and cause of death from the medical examiner."

"Then Steve is your main suspect," I said. "And I'd bet that Steve will try to dig up more graves to find the missing ring. That or he'll track it back to Rebecca and try to get the ring from her."

"I doubt he'd do that," Mike said. "He'll assume it's still buried in the ground."

"You're sure about that?" I asked. "You could set up a trap for him, you know. You could—"

"You might be onto something, but setting up a trap ain't gonna happen," he replied. "Not with Rourke around and not on such short notice. There's too much red tape for us to get through, unfortunately."

That was annoying.

"There's got to be something you can do," I said.

"Follow the leads and make an arrest," Mike replied. "You've done enough, Bee. You can relax. I've got this from here."

Mike was right. He was capable, he did good police work and he made great deductions, but something was off. "You don't have DNA or fingerprints or anything like that?"

He shook his head, pinching the bridge of his nose. "Whoever did this put a solid plan into place. I need that coroner's report before I can put a plan in place. Like I said. You can relax."

I nodded, rising from my seat. I tucked my handbag over my shoulder and smiled at him. "Thanks for everything you do, Mike. I know this has been a tough time for you."

He gave me a smile. "Appreciate that."

And then I left his office and moved through the police department and pushed my way through the glass front doors—scratched and in need of repair—and out into the sunlight. I still wasn't entirely sure where Mike and I stood romantically, but at least I had fixed things up "professionally."

Now came the challenge of letting this one go. He had it under control. We knew who the murderer was.

Then why did I feel like we didn't?

Twenty-Two

That afternoon...

I COULDN'T SHAKE THE FEELING THAT WE WERE wrong about Steve. It haunted my thoughts during the rest of the day, right up until we closed the bakery for the afternoon and headed home. Jamie was in his study, typing away, and Ruby was keen for rest and relaxation after what had been a fun and long day in the bakery.

She had regaled me with tales of the locals and tourists she had met along the way, and how people had grown increasingly frustrated with the lack of resolution in the grave robbing case. And now in Nate's murder case.

"Bee?"

I blinked out of my thoughts. "Yeah?" We were at the dining room table in the house, enjoying a glass of Jamie's homemade lemonade to wind down after work. It was hotter than a Carolina Reaper in Mystery today, and the lemonade and cool interior of the house was a welcome reprieve from the heat.

"What's going on?" Ruby scratched the underside of Cookie's ginger chin. "You seem so preoccupied. Is it the case?"

I nodded. "I went to see Mike today after I talked with Rebecca."

"Oh?"

I told her what had happened and how I felt about it, putting emphasis on my issue with Steve.

"What makes you think it's not him?" Ruby asked. "If all the evidence points in his direction, and it surely seems to, then he has to be the guy, right?"

"Yeah." I tapped my chin. "But if that's the case, why do I feel like we're so wrong about this?"

"You always tell me to trust my gut," Ruby replied. "So why wouldn't you do the same this time around?"

"Meaning what, exactly?"

"Let's take a walk down to the cemetery," she said. "We can take Caramel with, since he needs to stretch his legs. If Steve is there, you can ask him a couple of questions. Or maybe you can snoop around in that caretaker's hutch and see if there's anything there that pertains to the case."

That was a great idea. "I'm in," I said. "Give me a couple of minutes to get ready." I hurried out of the house and to my cottage.

I splashed water on my face to freshen up, slipped on a pair of walking shoes, and got Caramel ready for a walk. "Caramel," I said, "we've got to be smart about this. We have to find out what Steve is hiding, if he's hiding anything, and if he isn't... There will be other leads to investigate."

Caramel yipped approval. It was funny, but he'd started answering to the name I'd given him. I wasn't a great believer in fate, but it seemed I had been fated to find this dog and to care for him. Just like I had been fated to see the flashlights in the cemetery on that first night of the case.

We met up with Ruby in front of the house then started down the long dirt path that led out of the property that was, as the locals liked to tell us, "out there in the willywacks."

Half an hour later, after several stops to drink water in the shade of trees, and having filled a small water bowl for Caramel as well, we reached the cemetery.

The gates were open, as always, but a cursory glance inside didn't show us Steve or anything of note. We entered the cemetery, checked our sixes, and then headed for the caretaker's hutch. The wooden construction had a set of stairs leading up to its door—which was, I discovered upon a quick tug on the handle, firmly locked.

"The windows are locked too," Ruby observed, "and quite far off the ground."

"Where is Steve?" I muttered, staring up the path that led under the trees and past gravestones. A distant rumble of thunder rolled through the air. Clouds had gathered on the far horizon, blown in on the wind. A gentle breeze that smelled of coming rain brushed the hair from my face.

Caramel barked and whined.

"What's wrong?" I bent and picked him up. "What is it?"

He snuggled into my arms, trembling.

"Maybe he doesn't like the weather," Ruby said.

"Hmm." I stroked Caramel's soft ears and whispered sweet nothings to comfort him. He whined again. "I don't know. The last time he acted like this, it was on the night I—"

"Pookie?" The voice, feminine and brash, had come from the direction of the cemetery gates. "Pookie, is that you?"

Dewy Phillips stood there, curly hair framing her face, wearing a pair of slippers, jean shorts, and a strappy top.

She held a cigarette between her fingers, the ash leaning from the end, threatening to drop to the sidewalk.

"Dewy?" I held Caramel tighter. The dog whined and trembled then let out a bark.

"That's my dog," she said, pointing the cigarette at Caramel, the ash holding on still, burning lower and lower toward the filter. "You stole my dog!"

"I reported this dog missing," I said. "He's not microchipped."

"That's *my* Pookie." Dewy insisted, dropping the cigarette, ash and all, to the sidewalk and crushing it under foot. "Come here, Pookie. Here, boy." She patted her knees. "Come on. Come to, mama."

Caramel growled and hid his nose.

"Come on, you dubbah!" Dewy snapped that out.

"Don't you dare talk to him like that," I said, giving her the icy stare that struck fear into people's hearts. "Ever."

Dewy glared back at me, but saw the ill intent in my eyes. "Pookie?" A final try at getting my dog to come to her. "Pookie, come here right now."

"He doesn't want to live with you any more," I said. "He belongs to me now." It felt good to say it, albeit a little risky given the circumstances.

But the minute Dewy had said that Caramel was her dog, the iron weight in my belly had vanished, replaced by a certainty that I had been right. Steve wasn't the murderer. Dewy was. Her dog had been waiting outside the cemetery on the night of the murder. And she had come back to the scene of the crime.

Dewy mumbled something indistinct then made a very rude gesture in our direction. "Don't want that waste of space anyway," Dewy said. "He was a bad dog."

"You're a bad egg," I snapped. "And you'd better get out of here before you regret it."

"How dare you call him that," Ruby added in. "Rude, horrible woman. Go away!" She hardly ever got this mad. It was something to behold, Ruby with a snarl peeling her lips back over her teeth. She looked more ready to bite than Caramel was.

Dewy finally backed up. "Keep him then. Dubbahs." And off she went, back down the street.

"What a wretched woman," Ruby whispered, rubbing her arms to soothe herself. "To say that about poor Caramel…"

"She's the murderer," I said.

"W-What?"

"Think about it, Rubes. Caramel was here on the night of the grave robbing, and she's Nate's ex. She knew about the ring because she was there with him on the night of the party and she lived with him for Pete's sake."

Ruby swallowed. "So what do we do?"

"We set up a trap," I replied. "We set up a trap, tell Mike what's going on, and catch the person who started all of this."

"How?"

Caramel had relaxed in my arms now that Dewy was gone. "I know just the woman to call."

Twenty-Three

The following night, late...

THE TRAP HAD BEEN SET AS BEST AS WE COULD manage.

Ruby and I waited, hidden between the trees, watching opposite ends of the clearing that held Connie's grave. We waited in bated breath, our phones on silent but at the ready should we need to call each other or for help.

I had already talked to Mike about the plan this morning.

"Don't go ahead with this, Bee," Mike had said, loudly. "I can't approve of your actions on this one." And then he lowered his voice. "I'll send a car around

01:15 a.m. to check you're all right. That's the most I can do."

The cops couldn't officially go along with what we were doing. They didn't have warrants, nor could they "rely" on civilians like us, but that didn't matter. Mike would support us from afar, and we would catch Dewy in the act.

I shot off a text to Ruby. "It's quiet. Looks like they're done." I was hidden behind a tree further removed from Connie's gravestone, while Ruby had a closer view.

Her text blipped through on my screen. "Yeah. Mourners are heading out now."

The mourners in question were friends of Rebecca's.

Yesterday afternoon, in what I considered a stroke of genius, I had contacted Rebecca and asked her to hold a candlelight vigil for Connie because her grave had been disturbed. And then we'd spread the news as far and wide as possible, including the fact that Rebecca planned on leaving her sister's ring on her grave tonight.

The plan was to draw Dewy back to the cemetery and catch her in the act of trying to take the ring.

I checked the time—it was almost 01:00 a.m.. The vigil was over.

A text came through on my screen. "The decoy ring is in place. Rebecca is on her way out of the cemetery."

This was it. "Going dark," I texted back. "Suggest you

do the same. We can't afford to be seen because of the lights on our phones."

"Good luck." Ruby's text came back with a thumbs up emoji and a smiley face.

I tucked my phone into my pocket and waited for my eyes to adjust to the dark, pulling my balaclava down over my face. I'd recently bought one, and I regretted it. First, the thing was woolen and scratchy, and second, it was hot tonight—most unlike every other summer night we'd experienced so far, which were comfortably cool.

I couldn't understand why criminals would want to put themselves through this, but I'd do it to catch a killer.

The silence blossomed in the night, and I sweated angrily, peeking out at the gravestone which was, thankfully, white and plainly obvious in the moonlight.

A shadow moved in the darkness. Pale legs approached the gravestone, and the telltale sign of someone scraping their feet along the grass caught my ears. Definitely Dewy.

I counted to ten, watching the figure get closer and closer. Dewy paused every now and again, glancing around like a timid squirrel.

Finally, she bent to grab the ring. Her back was toward me.

I thundered out from behind the tree and sprinted toward her. I jumped and launched myself onto her back, sending her tumbling to the ground.

She let out a shriek and struggled against my grip, but Ruby appeared beside me and slipped one cable tie over Dewy's ankles and another over her wrists.

It was shockingly easy to take her by surprise and doubt flitted through my subconscious. I grabbed Dewy by the shoulders and propped her up against the grave, signaling for Ruby to bring out her flashlight.

My friend trembled, but directed the beam first into Dewy's eyes before shifting it over her shoulder and onto Connie's gravestone.

The fake ring lay discarded off to one side.

"Let me go!" Dewy whined, terror in her tone. "Please, let me go. I didn't do nothing. It wasn't me. It wasn't me, OK?"

I brought my phone out of my pocket and started recording the conversation. "You killed Nate."

"No, I didn't! I would never have done that. I loved Nate. I loved him."

"Then why did you try to steal Connie's ring?" I asked. "We know everything. We know about Nate's plan to steal the ring. We know you helped dig up the graves."

"No. Please."

"You'd better start talking," I said.

"Who are you?" Dewy's forehead was streaked with sweat, and her chin trembled. "I know you from somewhere?"

"Talk!" I shook a finger at her.

"I didn't do it," she said. "It wasn't me. Look, I don't know anything about anything. I just came here because… Because…"

"Because why?"

A siren whooped outside the cemetery gates once. The cavalry had arrived. I fully expected it would be Mike himself who had come to check what had transpired.

"Because Warner told me too," she wailed. "Warner said I should come fetch the ring. He said he would pay me back for all the money he owed me if I got the ring. That's all. I don't know anything about Nate or the grave robbing, I—"

"But you and Warner were together on the morning Nate went missing," Ruby put in. "Weren't you?"

"No," she whispered. "We weren't together. I went to SumFruit with him, but he left before me. I—I—I didn't know where he went. I don't ask Warner questions if I don't have to. He gets real mad."

"What about your dog?" I asked.

"Pookie?"

"Why was your dog at the cemetery on the night the graves were robbed?"

Her lower lip stiffened, and she shook her head. "Don't know what you're talking about."

I didn't buy it for a second. She knew *exactly* what I

was talking about, and she had come here to collect the ring because she wanted the riches it promised. Either she had killed Nate on her own or Warner had helped her. Either way, we had caught one of the perpetrators.

A flashlight beam swished across the cemetery toward us, and Mike strode into view. "Ah," he said. "You're here."

Mike drew me aside, out of earshot of Dewy while Ruby watched over her.

"She tried to take the ring," I said, pulling my balaclava up and off. I looked like a sweaty, drowned rat, but oh well. I could breathe. "She's claiming that Warner was the one who killed Nate."

"That's funny she said that," he whispered, his cologne drifting toward me and making me aware of how ridiculous I had to look, sweat-streaked and all dressed in black. "I've got Warner back in the interrogation room telling me the exact opposite. Pair of dubbahs decided to give the same alibi. They were in SumFruit. Coroner's report came back. Nate was poisoned and dumped in the ocean. They found traces of blueberry smoothie in his stomach. And the time of death corresponds with a time when neither of them had an alibi."

"Wow."

"Ayuh. We arrested Warner about an hour ago when we got the results. He's claiming Dewy came out here of her own accord. My bet is she came to get the ring and make a run for it. Leave her brother in prison to rot," he said.

So the three of them, Warner, Dewy, and Nate, had worked together to try to find the "hidden treasure", but had failed and started turning on each other.

"She'll sing once we tell her what her brother's been saying," Mike said. "Now, you two better get out of here before backup gets here. I've got to cuff her and remove the cable ties or you two will get in a mess of trouble with Rourke and the captain."

"Thanks, Mike."

He grinned at me. "Thank you," he replied, and then he put his arm around my waist, pulled me close, and placed a kiss on my lips.

It was over fast, but it left me reeling. It had been a long time since I'd kissed a man. The last had been my husband. And it had been equally long since a man had given me butterflies or intellectually challenged me.

Thankfully, it hadn't been that long since Ruby and I had solved yet another murder case.

Epilogue

Two weeks after the spectacular arrest of Warner and Dewy Phillips, and the tourism season in Mystery was in full swing. The grave robbing, murder, and arrests had made the town popular—because there were plenty of sickos in the world who were fascinated by murder cases. And I was one of them.

I hummed under my breath, dusting my floury hands off on my apron in the bakery kitchen, smiling at the dough I had brought together.

Things in my life had been coming together as well, and it was good to feel that way for a change.

"I still can't believe it was them," Leslie said, picking up on the thread of conversation we'd been having a few moments earlier. "I know it's been a couple of weeks, but it's just..."

"Crazy?"

"Ayuh. I knew Dewy and Warner, and they weren't exactly nice, but I didn't think they were... Y'know, murderers."

"Nobody did," I said. "That's the thing about murderers. You never see them coming. If you did, they wouldn't have the chance to get you."

Leslie shuddered and brought butter out of the fridge, placing it beside the stovetop. "I don't like the thought of that."

"Nobody does, but it's a fact of life. Dewy and Warner are firmly behind bars. They'll have their day in court."

The kitchen door opened, and Ruby peeped around it. "Bee?"

"Yeah?"

"There's someone out here to see you."

I set the dough aside to rise, then proceeded out into the dining area. It was early in the morning, and the first few customers had trickled in and sat at tables throughout the space. Mike, looking dapper in a buttoned shirt, his lanyard hanging around his neck, stood near the coffee machine, waiting with his hands in his pockets.

"Mike," I said, going over, the butterflies in my stomach popping into existence.

They returned whenever he was around or I so much as thought of him, the treacherous things. But, I was slowly learning to accept them, and the fact that I liked Mike. A lot. The last time I had liked a man this much, I had been a young woman and had wound up marrying the guy.

"'Chuppta?'" Mike's face split into a handsome grin.

"Oh, you know, baking and helping run a bakery."

Ruby excused herself from the conversation and went over to take a nearby table's order.

"Sounds like hard work. Want to blow off some steam tonight and watch a movie? I'll make popcorn. You can bring the wine."

"Sounds great," I said, blushing.

Mike swept a strand of hair behind my ear. "I've got good news."

"Oh yeah?"

"Ayuh. Rourke's gone back to Portland," he said.

"Fantastic."

"That's not all," he continued, taking a breath. "I managed to get the captain to open up Connie Gardener's old case. I'm going to be investigating it."

My heart swooped in my chest. "You're kidding!"

"I don't kid about murder," he replied somberly. "And I'd appreciate your expert opinion on the case too. We can discuss it over dinner before the movie. What do you say?"

"That would be fantastic, Mike. Amazing. I can't even..." I threw my arms around him and squeezed him tight, right there in front of the entire bakery. It was so unlike me, I snapped out of it quickly and placed my arms at my side, awkwardly after.

Mike let out a happy chuckle that made him sound a little like Santa Claus. The gray beard didn't help to dispel the effect.

"Well, all right then. Guess we'll be talking about it." Mike leaned in and brushed a kiss across my cheek before swaggering out of the bakery and into the street. He gave one last glance back at me, waved, and then got into his unmarked car and drove off.

Ruby let out a squeal beside me, and I jumped.

"Are you trying to scare the soul out of my body?" I gasped.

"Sorry, I thought you'd realize I was right next to you. But I guess you were too busy swooning over your handsome detective to notice."

Thankfully, my cheeks couldn't get any redder at this point. "I wasn't."

"You're a terrible liar," Ruby said. "And this is amazing, Bee. He wants you to help him. And he likes you. A lot."

"Well. That's... That's neither here nor there. I have bread to bake for a bread pudding. I—" And then I hurried off, hoping that everyone in the bakery hadn't witnessed my humiliation. But the joy soon overwhelmed my embarrassment.

Mike wanted my help. He respected my opinions. And he wanted to take me out tonight. Best of all, Ruby would be happy to look after my dear dog, Caramel, while I was gone.

It had all worked out, and life was getting better.

I had, after my husband's death, put myself up on the shelf when it came to men and relationships. I had been so certain that my romantic life was over, and that the most I could ever want was friendships and professional success.

Tears ran down my cheeks.

Two arms encircled me in the kitchen, and I found Ruby hugging me from behind her head resting on my shoulder. "You're wonderful, Bee," she whispered. "You deserve this."

"Thank you." Joy swelled in my chest.

"And by the way," she said, with a giggle. "Jamie and I are pregnant."

Ruby and Bee's adventures will continue soon! Keep and eye out for updates about the next Bee's Bakery Cozy Mystery. Join my mailing list here to have your say about the books. Do you think Bee's Bakery should be written from Bee's perspective? Or would you prefer to hear from Ruby? I'd love to hear your thoughts.

Craving More Cozy Mystery?

If you had fun with Ruby and Bee, you'll, love getting to know Charlie Mission and her butt-kicking grandmother, Georgina. You can read the first chapter of Charlie's story, *The Case of the Waffling Warrants,* below!

"Come in, Big G, come in." I spoke under my breath so that the flesh-colored microphone seated against my throat picked up my voice. "What is your status?"

My grandmother, Georgina—pet name Gamma, code name Big G—was out on a special operation. Reconnaissance at the newest guesthouse in our town, Gossip. The reason? First, she was an ex-spy, as was I, and second, the woman who'd opened the guesthouse was her mortal enemy and in direct competition with my grandmother's establishment, the Gossip Inn.

Who was this enemy, this bringer of potential financial doom?

A middle-aged woman with a penchant for wearing pashminas and annoying anyone who looked her way.

Jessie Belle-Blue.

It was rumored that even thinking the woman's name summoned a murder of crows.

"I repeat, Big G, what is your status?"

"I'm en route to the nest," my grandmother replied in my earpiece.

I let out a relieved sigh and exited my bedroom, heading downstairs to help with the breakfast service.

In the nine months since I had retired as a spy, life in Gossip had been normal. In the Gossip sense of the term. I'd expected that my job as a server, maid, and assistant would bring the usual level of "cat herding" inherent when working at the inn. Whether that involved tracking down runaway cats, literally, or providing a guest with a moist towelette after a fainting spell—tempers ran high in Gossip.

What was the reason for the craziness? Shoot, it had to be something in the water.

I took the main stairs two at a time and found my friend, the inn's chef, paging through her recipe book in the lime green kitchen. Lauren Harris wore her red hair in a French braid today, apron stretched over her pregnant belly.

"Morning," I said, "how are you today?"

"Madder than a fat cat on a diet." She slapped her recipe book closed and turned to me.

Uh oh. Looks like it's time for more cat herding.

"What's wrong?"

"My supplier is out of flour and sugar. Can you believe that?" Lauren huffed, smoothing her hands over her belly while the clock on the wall ticked away. Breakfast was in two hours and Lauren loved baking cupcakes as part of the meal.

"Do you have enough supplies to make cupcakes for this morning?"

"Yes. But just for today," Lauren replied. "The guests are going to love my new waffle cupcakes, and they'll be sore they can't get anymore after this batch is done. Why, I should go down there and wring Billy's neck for doing this to me. He knows I take an order of sugar and flour every week, and I get it at just above cost too. What's Georgina going to say?"

"Don't stress, Lauren," I said. "We'll figure it out."

"Right." She brightened a little. "I nearly forgot you're the one who "fixes" things around here." Lauren winked at me.

She was the only person in the entire town who knew that my grandmother and I had once been spies for the NSIB—the National Security Investigative Bureau. But the news that I had helped solve several murders had spread through town, and now, anybody and everybody with a problem would call me up asking for help. A lot of them offered me money. And I was selective about who I chose to help.

"I'll check it out for you if you'd like," I said. "The flour issue."

"Nah, that's OK. I'm sure Billy will get more stock this week. I'll lean on him until he squeals."

"Sounds like you've been picking up tips from Georgina."

Lauren giggled then returned to her super-secret recipe book—no one but she was allowed to touch it.

"What's on the menu this morning?" I asked.

Lauren was the boss in the kitchen—she told me what to do, and I followed her instructions precisely. If I did anything else, like trying to read the recipe for instance, the food would end up burned, missing ingredients or worse.

The only place I wasn't a "fixer" was in the Gossip Inn's kitchen.

"Bacon and eggs over easy, biscuits and gravy, waffle cupcakes and... oh, I can't make fresh baked bread, can I?"

"Tell her I'll bring some back with me from the

bakery." Gamma's voice startled me. Goodness, I'd forgotten about the earpiece—she could hear everything happening in the kitchen.

"I'll text Georgina and ask her to bring bread from the bakery."

"You're a lifesaver, Charlotte."

We set to work on the breakfast—it was 7:00 a.m. and we needed everything done within two hours—and fell into our easy rhythm of baking and cooking.

My grandmother entered the kitchen at around 8:30 a.m., dressed in a neat silk blouse and a pair of slacks rather than the black outfit she'd left in for her spy mission. Tall, willowy, and with neatly styled gray hair, Gamma had always reminded me of Helen Mirren playing the Queen.

"Good morning, ladies," she said, in her prim, British accent. "I bring bread and tidings."

"What did you find out?" I asked.

"No evidence of the supposed ghost tours," Gamma said.

We'd started hosting ghost tours at the inn recently, so of course Jessie Belle-Blue wanted to do the same. She was all about under-cutting us, but, thankfully, the Gossip Inn had a legacy and over 1,000 positive reviews on Trip-Advisor.

Breakfast time arrived, and the guests filled the quaint dining area with its glossy tables, creaking wooden floors, and egg yolk yellow walls. Chatter and laughter leaked through the swinging kitchen doors with their porthole windows.

"That's my cue," I said, dusting off my apron, and heading out into the dining room.

I picked up a pot of coffee from the sideboard where we kept the drinks station and started my rounds.

Most of the guests had gathered around a center table in the dining room, and bursts of laughter came from the group, accompanied by the occasional shout.

I elbowed my way past a couple of guests—nobody could accuse me of having great people skills—apologizing along the way until I reached the table. The last time something like this had happened, a murder had followed shortly afterward.

Not this time. No way.

"—the last thing she'd ever hear!" The woman seated at the table, drawing the attention, was vaguely familiar. She wore her dark hair in luscious curls, and tossed it as she spoke, looking down her upturned nose at the people around the table.

"What happened then, Mandy?" Another woman asked, her hands clasped together in front of her stomach.

Mandy? Wait a second, isn't this Mandy Gilmore?

Gamma had mentioned her once before—Mandy was

a massive gossip in town. Why wasn't she staying at her house?

"What happened? Well, she ran off with her tail between her legs, of course. She'll soon learn not to cross me. Heaven knows, I always repay my debts."

"What, like a Lannister from *Game of Thrones*?" That had come from a taller woman with ginger curls.

"Shut up, Opal," Mandy replied. "You have no idea what we're talking about, and even if you did, you wouldn't have the intelligence to comprehend it."

The crowd let out various 'oofs' in response to that. The woman next to me clapped her hand over her mouth.

"You're all talk, Gilmore." Opal lifted a hand and yammered it at the other woman. "You act like you're a threat, but we know the truth around here."

"The truth?" Mandy leaned in, pressing her hands flat onto the tabletop, the crystal vase in the center rattling. "And what's that, Opal, darling? I'd love to hear it."

"That you're a failure. You sold your house, left Gossip with your head in the clouds, told everyone you were going to become a successful businesswoman, and now you're back. Back to scrape together the pieces of the life you have left."

"Witch!" Mandy scraped her chair back.

"All right, all right," I said, setting down the coffee pot

on the table. "That's enough, ladies. Everyone head back to their tables before things get out of hand."

Both Opal and Mandy stared daggers at me.

I flashed them both smiles. "We wouldn't want to ruin breakfast, would we? Lauren's prepared waffle cupcakes."

That distracted them. "Waffle cupcakes?" Opal's brow wrinkled. "How's that going to work?"

"Let's talk about it at your table." I grabbed my coffee pot and walked her away from Mandy. The crowd slowly dispersed, people muttering regret at having missed out on a show. The Gossip Inn was popular for its constant conflict.

If the rumors didn't start here then they weren't worth repeating. That was the mantra, anyway.

I seated Opal at her table, and she pursed her lips at me. "You shouldn't have interrupted. That woman needs a piece of my mind."

"We prefer peace of mind at the inn." I put up another of my best smiles.

Compared to what I'd been through in the past— hiding out from my rogue spy ex-husband and eventually helping put him behind bars when he found me—dealing with the guests was a cakewalk.

"What brings you to Gossip, Opal?" I asked.

"I live here," she replied, waspishly. "I'm staying here while they're fumigating my house. Roaches."

"Ah." I struggled not to grimace. Thankfully, my cell phone buzzed in the front pocket of my apron and distracted me. "Coffee?"

"I don't take caffeine." And she said it like I'd offered her an illegal substance too.

"Call me if you need anything." I hurried off before she could make good on that promise, bringing my phone out of my pocket.

I left the coffee pot on the sideboard, moving into the Gossip Inn's spacious foyer, the chandelier overhead off, but catching light in glimmers. The tables lining the hall were filled with trinkets from the days when the inn had been a museum—an eclectic collection of bits and bobs.

"This is Charlotte Smith," I answered the call—I would never get to use my true last name, Mission, again, but it was safer this way.

"Hello, Charlotte." A soft, rasping voice. "I've been trying to get through to you. I'm desperate."

"Who is this?"

"My name is Tina Rogers, and I need your help."

"My help."

"Yes," she said. "I understand that you have a certain set of skills. That you fix people's problems?"

"I do. But it depends on the problem and the price." I didn't have a set fee for helping people, but if it drew me away from the inn for long, I had to charge. I was technically a consultant now. Sort of like a P.I. without the fedora and coffee-stained shirt.

"My mother will handle your fee," Tina said. "I've asked her to text you about it, but I... I don't have long to talk. They're going to pull me off the phone soon."

"Who?"

"The police," she replied. "I'm calling you from the holding cell at the Gossip Police Station. I've been arrested on false charges, and I need you to help me prove my innocence."

"Miss Rogers, it's probably a better idea to invest in a lawyer." But I was tempted. It had been a long time since I'd felt useful.

"No! I'm not going to a lawyer. I'm going to make these idiots pay for ever having arrested me."

I took a breath. "OK. Before I accept your... case, I'll need to know what happened. You'll need to tell me everything." I glanced through the open doorway that led into the dining room. No one looked unhappy about the lack of service yet.

"I can't tell you everything now. I don't have much time."

"So give me the *CliffsNotes*."

"I was arrested for breaking into and vandalizing Josie Carlson's bakery, The Little Cake Shop. Apparently, they found my glove there—it was specially embroidered, you see—but it's not mine because—" The line went dead.

"Hello? Miss Rogers?" I pulled the cellphone away from my ear and frowned at the screen. "Darn."

My interest was piqued. A mystery case about a break-in that involved the local bakery? Which just so happened to be run by one of my least favorite people in Gossip?

And when I'd just started getting bored with the push and pull of everyday life at the inn?

Count me in.

Want to read more? You can grab **the first book** in *the Gossip Cozy Mystery series* on all major retailers.

Happy reading, friend!

Paperbacks Available by Rosie A. Point

A Burger Bar Mystery series

The Fiesta Burger Murder

The Double Cheese Burger Murder

The Chicken Burger Murder

The Breakfast Burger Murder

The Salmon Burger Murder

The Cheesy Steak Burger Murder

A Bite-sized Bakery Cozy Mystery series

Murder by Chocolate

Marzipan and Murder

Creepy Cake Murder

Murder and Meringue Cake

Murder Under the Mistletoe

Murder Glazed Donuts

Choc Chip Murder

Macarons and Murder

Candy Cake Murder

Murder by Rainbow Cake

Murder With Sprinkles

Trick or Murder

Christmas Cake Murder

S'more Murder

Murder and Marshmallows

Donut Murder

Buttercream Murder

Chocolate Cherry Murder

Caramel Apple Murder

Red, White 'n Blue Murder

Pink Sprinkled Murder

Murder by Milkshake

Murder by Cupid Cake

Caramel Cupcake Murder

Cake Pops and Murder

Chicken Murder Soup

Murderoni and Cheese

Lemon Murder Pie

A Gossip Cozy Mystery series

The Case of the Waffling Warrants

The Case of the Key Lime Crimes

The Case of the Custard Conspiracy

A Mission Inn-possible Cozy Mystery series

Vanilla Vendetta

Strawberry Sin

Cocoa Conviction

Mint Murder

Raspberry Revenge

Chocolate Chills

A Very Murder Christmas series

Dachshund Through the Snow

Owl Be Home for Christmas

Made in the USA
Las Vegas, NV
05 August 2024